TENDERFOOT ON THE TRAIL

Robert Malkovitch was brought up on the mean streets of New York. When he saves a newspaper editor from a street mugging, his life changes and he becomes an apprentice reporter. Six months later, he goes west to report on conditions for would-be immigrants. So begins his initiation into an entirely new life where justice is carried out with rope and bullet. It isn't long before Robert kills his first man — an outlaw from the Falco gang. Now the hunt is on . . .

TEX LARRIGAN

TENDERFOOT ON THE TRAIL

Complete and Unabridged

LINFORD
Leicester

First published in Great Britain in 2002 by
Robert Hale Limited
London

First Linford Edition
published 2004
by arrangement with
Robert Hale Limited
London

British Library CIP Data

Larrigan, Tex
    Tenderfoot on the trail.—Large print ed.—
Linford western library
1. Large type books
2. Western stories
I. Title
823.9'14 [F]

ISBN 1–84395–169–X

Published by
F. A. Thorpe (Publishing)
Anstey, Leicestershire

Set by Words & Graphics Ltd.
Anstey, Leicestershire
Printed and bound in Great Britain by
T. J. International Ltd., Padstow, Cornwall

This book is printed on acid-free paper

1

Robert Malkovitch whistled as he hurried through the back lane behind the offices of the *New York Tribune*. He was late and he hoped to sneak in the back way and be at his desk before the boss realized he'd been missing for the last half-hour.

He'd slept in, because he'd been out most of the night on a story. He was pleased with himself. The cops had allowed him to tag along and all because he'd been the one to find the girl with her throat cut in an alley behind the saloon. He'd only found her because he'd wanted to pee and the usual place was stinking so he'd stepped into the shadows of the alley. He'd been nearly sick when he'd seen the stark white face and the puddle of blood. He'd stepped in it before he'd been aware of what it was.

He'd not had time to write up his report and he'd have to get to it now. The editor, Bill Mayfield, was apt to roar for him at any time. He wanted this scoop to be successful and make up for the stupid mistake of last week. He shuddered and tried to forget that dressing-down he'd got in front of the other grinning reporters, just because he'd rushed off to a robbery and got the address wrong and the details had been splashed out in an extra edition put out by their rivals at the *New York Journal*.

He slipped through the back door and at once his ears were deafened by the printing machine going full blast. There was the smell of oil and ink, which always excited him. He made his way to the typesetting room and old Joe looked up with inky fingers and gave him a nod.

'No need to rush, Malko,' old Joe shouted, he having been deaf for years through the constant racket. 'Bill knows you're late. He's been yelling for you for hours!'

'He can't have been! I'm only half an hour late!'

'He was here at the crack of dawn. Caught some of the nighthawks messing about and he's in a rare temper. I'd advise you to watch yourself!'

Robert groaned. There was no time to stop and talk. He rushed by and galloped along a dark corridor and into the reporters' room. He slid into his seat, sweating a little. He pulled his notes from his pocket and got down to a graphic account of what he'd seen and what had been done the night before.

He was half-way through his piece when the glass door of the editor's office was flung open and Bill Mayfield was roaring like a bull.

'Where the hell is Malkovitch? I'll skin the goddamn hide off him when he turns himself in!'

Heads lifted, scribbling ceased and all heads turned to Robert. He stood up slowly, hearing a snigger behind him. So the end had come. He hadn't lasted long, only six months as an apprentice reporter and he'd had such dreams of being an ace correspondent. He wouldn't even get a job on the *Journal* because Bill Mayfield knew Oscar Cole who ran the *Journal* with a rod of iron and he couldn't stand latecomers.

Slowly, with head down, he made his way towards the editor who glared at him as if he was some new species of cockroach.

'Come in here, I want to talk to you, and shut the door quietly. I don't want to have to deduct the price of new glass off your pay.'

So that was it. He was getting the push.

Bill Mayfield settled his bulk behind his desk and lit a cheap cigar which made Robert cough. He tried to suppress the cough and only made things worse. Oh, what the hell, what did it matter? He'd soon be gone and back in the Bronx, just another kid trying to make something of himself and not succeeding.

It had been a feather in his cap when Bill Mayfield had offered him a job one night when the man had been drinking. He'd been mugged and Robert had been there. He'd seen Jake Harris give Mayfield a right clout on the head, drop him and reach expertly for his wallet.

Robert had never liked Jake Harris. He was a bully, a few years older than himself and had terrorized all the kids on the block for years. Now he could get his own back. He'd hit Jake with a brick and felled him. Then he'd helped Mayfield to his feet, dusted the man down and returned his wallet to him.

Mayfield had been grateful and gave him five bucks.

'What's a boy like you doing around here?'

'Making a living as best as I can.'

'What can you do?'

'Most anything, I guess. Run errands, serve in the saloon when they're busy. Keep order when the rowdies are in on a Saturday night and I can write and figure. My pa was a teacher before he died. I got some education, and I can look after cab horses, feeding and minding them. You know, the usual thing.'

'Mmm, not bad. How would you like to work for me?'

Robert had stared at him, surprised.

'You mean real work, not odd jobs?'

'Yes, real work. I'm the editor of the *New York Tribune* and I think you've the makings of a good reporter. You seem bright and an opportunist. Well? What do you say?'

And that was how Robert Malkovitch got his first real job at twenty years old.

Now he stood before Bill Mayfield's desk and thought to himself, it had all been too good to last. He panicked a little. He'd bought a new suit from the little Jewish tailor in the same mean street where he rented a room in Mrs Barnes's boarding house. He'd got it on the understanding he could pay for it weekly. He still owed old Reuben half the dough.

'Sit down,' Bill Mayfield said testily.

'Don't stand there as if the end of the world is nigh!'

Robert collapsed on the hard wooden chair and waited while Mayfield got his cigar going good and proper.

Robert remembered his half-written article. If he got that information over, he might just save his job.

'Sorry I was late in, Mr Mayfield, sir. I got me a scoop. I was the one who found that girl with her throat cut and I was up all night with the police hunting clues and such.'

'What girl?'

'Oh, you don't know? A prostitute called Annie was attacked after she'd had it off with some redneck who cut her throat afterwards and made off with what cash she had on her. Her room-mate swears she had twenty bucks on her, her night's takings. You know!'

Mayfield nodded. 'Yes, I do know. She'd been in the alley several times and someone somewhere didn't like her getting all the trade. I've heard it all before. She's not the first to be cut up just because she was successful!'

Robert felt a little deflated. It didn't sound so important when Mayfield told the tale.

'I've nearly finished an article about it. I'll put it on your desk as soon as it's finished.'

'Yes, well you do that. But what I want to talk to you about is what d'you think about going out West and reporting back to me what's going on out there? You're a smart lad and if you want to get on, it's experience you want. The other reporters are too old and set in their ways and some are married and don't want to go out West. Now, there's no one to stop you. You haven't got a girlfriend, have you?'

Robert blushed.

'Not a proper girlfriend, just someone I . . . '

'You needn't go on. I get the picture. Now what do you say to a raise in salary and expense money? Make no mistake, it'll be tough and you'll be like all those new migrants who're going out there with as little experience as yourself. You can keep a diary of the pitfalls and dangers that you'll face and I'll want you to wire me every two weeks. Is that understood?'

'Just a minute. I haven't said I'll go yet!'

'Well, if you don't, you're fired! It's your choice. I don't like latecomers, not even if they're up all night working on behalf of the newspaper. So what's it to be, eh?'

Robert stared at him blankly.

'I've only got my good suit. Old Reuben won't like it if I ruin it out West!'

Bill Mayfield laughed.

'I think the *New York Tribune* can afford to rig you out in something more casual, like a couple of flannel shirts, some denims and a leather jacket. Oh, and a hat and boots.'

'What about a gun? I've never handled a gun but I really think I should have one.'

'I don't see why not. We can't have our newspaper representative going out there without some means of protection.'

Robert swallowed.

'What about a horse? I've never rode before.'

'Look, you get rigged out and we'll give you an extra two hundred bucks to take with you. We'll get you a ticket to ride on the new railroad to its terminus and from there, you can dicker about getting a horse. It will be up to you.'

'Where am I heading for?'

Bill Mayfield waved his hands vaguely.

'I don't know. Abilene's been mentioned but the new cattle town is Wichita. You've got a free range. Just get out there and send some good reports back so that a lot of these emigrants who keep pouring into our country have some idea of what they will face when they go West.'

He stood up, came round the desk and put an arm about Robert's shoulders. It lay heavily on him.

'Now my boy, I'm putting all my trust in you as if you were my own son. I know you'll do more than your best. You're smart and the kind of man they're looking for out in that great wilderness. You might even make your fortune. They say there's gold for the taking in the rivers out there. You could come back here and buy up the newspaper and I'd be working for you!'

Robert's eyes widened. It was a joke of course, but wouldn't it be a turn-up if he did just that?

A week later, he was ready to travel with all his wordly possessions stuffed into a carpetbag and a new belt and holster hung at his waist, loaded up with the old navy gun which he'd been too scared to try out at the pawn-broker's store. Soon he'd be gone.

2

Angus D. McAndrew, owner of the *New York Tribune* and a major shareholder in the Great Interstate Railway Company looked over his glasses and across his desk at Bill Mayfield, managing director and editor of his newspaper.

'So he got away then?'

'Yes. I saw him off myself.'

'You think he can keep one step ahead of the opposition?'

'I'm sure of it. The *Journal*'s sending Myers and we all know what an old fogey he is. Malkovitch is smart and he's got the fresh approach of youth. That's what we want here. He's got enthusiasm, has the kid. His stuff was a bit over the top here. Sometimes he went from fact to fiction which was embarrassing at times, but if he sends back accounts from the other side of the country, who's to tell fact from fiction? The readers will lap it all up. It'll read like some boy's adventure diary. You'll see.'

'Huh! I hope you're right. We don't want to become a laughing stock.'

'No fear of that. I'm going to edit his stuff myself. By the way, it was a great idea of yours to give him a railway pass, so he could get around without running out of funds.'

'Wouldn't be feasible any other way. You don't get far on a horse if you're tracking down stories. You said he'd never been on a horse, or fired a gun?'

'Yes, a pity and all that, but it makes it more interesting. There'll be lots of young fellers going West who're just as ignorant as he is. I'm looking forward to seeing how he copes.'

'You're a sadistic bastard, Bill. How would you feel if he was your son?'

'Well, he's not. He's a tough sonofabitch from the Bronx. He can use his fists and he's got a good head on his shoulders. That's why I chose him.'

'Mmm, well let's hope everything goes as you expect. Care for a drink and a cigar?'

'Now that's an offer I can't refuse!'

★ ★ ★

The train chugged on and on and the wheels clattering over the rails seemed to beat out a soporific rhythm which made Robert Malkovitch sleepy. The first euphoria had evaporated. He'd inspected the two passenger coaches, one for rich travellers and the other for the *hoi polloi* as he put it to himself.

There were upwards of twenty passengers sharing his coach. They consisted of half a dozen cowboys with their boss, obviously taking an easy ride home after driving cattle; a clergyman who kept his head in his Bible, a drummer who tried to sell the clergyman bottles of whiskey and proceeded every now and then to taste his own

14

wares. He made the whole coach smell like a saloon.

His eyes roamed over a fat couple who looked middle class, like a banker and his wife or a storekeeper and his lady. Then his eyes rested on the two flashy females with low-cut gowns covered carelessly by shawls. It made a feller feel hot down below when the shawls slipped and a bit of flesh was exposed. Hot stuff they were. He wondered whether he could include them in his notes. He also wondered how far they were going.

Then there were the odd ones, including a man dressed all in black wearing well-worn holsters like he knew how to use them. He slept most of the time with his Stetson over his eyes. Obviously he was used to this new kind of travel and the West was familiar to him. There was a little feller in a store suit and a derby hat and he looked out of place. He'd nearly chosen a derby himself when he'd bought his hat and now he was glad he hadn't. The feller looked a fool. He couldn't place him, not until later when the man produced a pack of cards and challenged the cowboys to play poker.

He dismissed the other two ladies as being school-ma'ams. They had stern downturned mouths, as if they disapproved of everything they saw.

He sighed and looked out of the window. As they rounded a curve he could see the long line of cattle-wagons lumbering behind.

There was also the smell of stewing beef in the restaurant car. It made his guts rumble. He sure would be glad when the waiter announced that it was chow-time.

There was one man left to study and he sat nearly opposite to Robert. This was the kind of man Robert reckoned all Western men should look like. He was dressed in soft leather pants and wore a fringed jerkin. His hair was long and coarse, blue-black in colour and he wore a ragged red sweatband around his forehead under a dirty stained hat that had had its shape punched out of it. What was more impressive, he wore two long Peacemakers in well-greased holsters and by his side was propped up a businesslike rifle. Robert didn't recognize what kind it was, and he was keen to ask but the man's hard visage didn't encourage conversation.

Robert's eyes turned to him more and more. Was he a famous gunman? An outlaw with enough nerve to ride the rails? Or was he a famous marshal? Robert's imagination was running riot.

The chow-bell rang and there was a sudden surge of activity as most of the passengers made for the small compartment at the back of their coach where a couple of sweating cooks were ready to dish up beef stew, hunks of bread and hot strong coffee.

Robert hung back and noticed that the man opposite him did the same. The mystery man smiled amusedly at Robert.

'Let the hungry mob get in first. They get the bare ration. Later, there's a lot left and latecomers get extra!' He winked and his dark visage changed.

Robert warmed to him. He laughed.

'I never thought of that. What if you're wrong and the grub runs out?'

The man shrugged.

'You lose some, you win some. A feller has to do with bread then. Still, that's better than being stuck in the desert without food and water!'

Robert looked at him curiously.

'Have you been stuck without food and water?'

'By God, yes! Many a time my guts were stuck to my backbone and my tongue swelled and turned black and I crawled on my hands and knees sniffing hard to smell water!'

'But you're still here. How come?'

Again the man laughed.

'Son, if you've fought the desert and the wastelands as long as I have, you find ways and means of survival. You look for the juicy cactus, you watch the terrain for signs of greenery and you know that down there under the ground could be a spring. You look for mud-wallows and follow the spoor of the animals. Then there's roots and grubs to be found, and of course there's the snakes and the small rodents that come out at night.'

Robert was itching to get out his notebook and write everything down. His eyes were wide as he listened, fascinated.

'You're not having me on? You really eat snakes?'

'Of course. They make good eating, especially when your stomach thinks your throat's cut!'

Robert took a deep breath.

'I don't think I could face eating a snake, especially raw.'

'You would, son, if it meant life or death.'

For several minutes they both sat quiet, Robert imagining himself skinning and eating such a repulsive thing and the mystery man thinking his own thoughts. Then he turned to Robert,

'This your first trip out West?'

'Yes.'

'Where you aiming for?'

Robert lifted his shoulders. 'Anywhere interesting. To the end of the line,'

'And then?'

'Get me a horse and maybe hitch on to some wagon train.'

'You'll have to be more specific, son. Will you be looking for gold or are you wanting to settle down in some fertile valley and learn ranching? Being a cowpoke is something a man learns as soon as he can walk. Can you shoot that there pistol?'

Robert felt his face flush. The man was making him feel a fool, an inexperienced tenderfoot.

'Yes,' he lied boldly, 'I can shoot.'

'Well, that's something in your favour. A feller's committing suicide if he thinks he can go West and not be able to shoot straight.'

Robert coughed. This son of a bitch was making him uneasy. He wondered if Bill Mayfield had deliberately sent him on this mission to get rid of him permanently.

Their talk was interrupted as the two maiden ladies returned from the cook-car with flushed faces.

'How disgusting!' one of them was saying indignantly to the other. 'Those two females making up to those cowboys and their ribald remarks! They made me feel real faint!'

'Now don't take on, Emma,' soothed the other. 'They'll get what they deserve. You mark my words!' They made their way to their seats. Emma fumbled in her reticule and produced a fan.

'Sluts!' she said viciously. 'No wonder ladies like ourselves are laid open to all kinds of treatment from coarse men! I tell you, Sarah, we'll have to be extra careful or we might be raped . . . ' her companion gave a little scream at the word . . . 'or even murdered and thrown off the train!'

'Ooh! It couldn't come to that, could it?'

'You never know,' Emma said darkly. 'We're travelling in a land of beasts!'

'Oh, I wish we'd never said we'd organize the school in Conyer's Butte. We should have stayed in New York!'

Emma went on fanning herself.

'Make no mistake, Sarah, we'll instil some discipline into those children out there and in time we'll influence their parents so they become civilized. We're being sent by the Lord, remember.'

Robert and the mystery man looked at each other and Robert saw the quirk of laughter fluttering at the corners of the man's mouth. The man got up from his seat and stretched.

'Time we ate, buddy. By the way, I'm Steve Caulfield. Just call me Steve.'

'I'm Robert Malkovitch, known as Malko.'

'Glad to know you, Malko.' They shook hands. 'Let's go see if I'm right about those cooks.'

They found some of the passengers still eating, others finished and sitting talking. Robert was amazed that Steve was right and as they carried their bowls and bread to an empty table there were curious and envious eyes watching the steaming piles of food.

'Say, how come you get extra?' a cowboy shouted at them. Steve grinned.

'We're clearing up the leavings. Any objections?'

The loud-mouthed cowboy looked Steve up and down and noted the Peacemakers.

'Nope! Just curious.'

'Good. If you have any grudge, take it up with the cooks!'

Steve sat down and attacked the stew as if his guts had been stuck to his backbone as he'd described earlier. Robert cautiously tasted his. He wondered which part of the cow he was eating, but it tasted good and he finally finished off his bowl, swiped it around with the last of his bread and left the bowl clean.

They lingered over their coffee and it was then, when all the passengers had returned to the main part of the coach, that Robert finally told Steve that he was a reporter for the *New York Tribune* and was on an assignment for that newspaper.

Steve was impressed. 'So you can read and write?'

Robert had to prove it by bringing out his notebook and showing him the contents. Steve looked blankly at it.

'Can't read any of it. Never had much schooling myself, but I sure can read sign, which is more important, I think.'

Robert nodded soberly. He'd never thought of that. He'd always considered himself superior to the ragged-assed toughs in the Bronx who'd had no inclinations to learn anything other than how to survive in the mean streets of New York.

Now, he supposed, they would be the equivalent of this man sitting opposite. But there was a difference, he instinctively knew that. This man could survive nature itself just to remain alive. The other sons of bitches survived by climbing on the backs of others. There was a savagery in them, which he'd learned to live with all his life. The experience had made him the tough fighting machine that he was, hiding behind the new Western gear and the notebook. Maybe he would surprise this Steve yet!

They both visited the two small cubicles that were situated between the coach proper and the cook-car. They each contained a wooden box-seat and a hole in the floor from which one could see the rail spars flash past as the train rocked from side to side. There was a small mirror on the wall and a tin washbasin with a plug and a metal container above it with a tap for cold water to wash with. Very necessary for these long journeys going West.

There was an atmosphere of tension when both men re-entered their coach. Robert, following Steve, saw him stiffen and his right hand flexed as he moved slowly forward.

Their way was blocked by the little

derby-hatted man in the store suit. He looked angry and was mouthing drunken curses at the cowboys who had been settling down to another poker session.

'You sons of bitches! Aren't I good enough to play with you bastards? Let me tell you, I've played with some of the best players in the country! There's seven of you. Why can't I make up another table and we'll all get down to some serious play!'

The ranch boss slowly got to his feet.

'Look, feller, are you deaf or something? Can't you get it into your thick head we don't want to play with you!'

'You're yeller, that's it! Won't take a chance on a good player!'

'Goddammit! Sit down before I lose patience,' growled the boss. 'It's a free country and if the boys don't want to play with you, that's it!'

'You're a lot of dadblasted gutless jaspers, if you let your boss dictate what you do!' The derby-hatted man took a swig from a half-empty whiskey bottle. 'I've half a mind to . . . '

None of them heard what he'd had a mind to do for Steve stepped up and cold-cocked him with his gun from behind. The man didn't know what had hit him but collapsed in a heap at Steve's feet.

Steve touched him with his foot but the man did not stir.

'A pity I had to do that, gentlemen and ladies, but the danger's over. I suspect he's got a derringer tucked away in his vest pocket.' Sure enough, as Robert stared, fascinated, Steve riffled through the pockets expertly and came up with an ugly-snouted pistol that was designed to fit snugly in the palm of the hand.

Everyone breathed a sigh of relief and relaxed. Steve smiled at Robert as they heaved the man upright, dumped him down in his seat, then sought their own.

'Lesson number one, Malko. Never take a man at face value out in the

West, and never ask questions. Just because you see a man not wearing a gun doesn't mean he hasn't one on his person somewhere. It might be in his sock or tucked in his belt at his back or up his sleeve. Always be cautious. Remember, a man who talks too much never listens!'

Robert nodded, suddenly subdued. He glanced at the man in the derby hat, still out, his head lolling. He'd have a hell of a sore head when he came to. He'd thought the man looked ridiculous but unassuming. How wrong he'd been. He wondered just how wrong he was about the rest of the passengers.

His eyes lighted on the man in black who was now awake and watching everyone closely. It was the first time Robert had seen his face. He wore an aggressive black beard and sideburns and his dark eyes glittered with some inner amusement. Come to think about it, he'd been the only one who'd not appeared apprehensive at the rantings of that drunken fool.

Now he studied the man and noticed that everything about the man was black, even his belt-buckle was not the usual silver-chased wrought piece that cowboys loved to wear. His hatband too, was plain and well worn. Everything about the man was geared to fast response and he wore his guns tied down below his knees. Surely Robert had heard of men like these who were fast-draw experts? He'd heard tales from some of the older reporters on the *Tribune*. They were the dangerous ones, the unpredictable screwballs who killed for the love of it, or so those reporters said, and they couldn't all have been pulling his leg. He swallowed and was thankful Steve Caulfield had taken him under his wing. Steve leaned towards him so that he could whisper in his ear.

'That feller you're studying, is a mercenary, I'll lay my last dollar on it. You can recognize them because they have nothing on them that can be used as a target. See what I mean? He can hide in the shadows and if he's good at his job he can be in quick and out again before anyone knows he's around. He'll not only be good with a gun but he'll be lethal with a knife. Look at his back when you get the opportunity and you'll see a slight bulge, hardly noticeable if you're not looking for it, down his back. That's where he hangs his shiv.'

'Shiv?'

'Yes, his shiv, knife if you like. Watch out if a man lifts his hand to his head. He's not going louse-hunting, he's probably going to stick you with his knife! And he can do it before you can blink. So beware!'

Robert looked at the man in black with more respect. He'd be glad when he came to the end of the line, which was at least another three days' travel. He was sick of the eternal jolting and the soot in the air from the belching chimney stack which meant no fresh air unless you chose to climb on to the observation platform outside and endure the taste of smoke and soot. He was also sick of the tension. The outburst from the derby-hatted man had not dissipated it. Everyone seemed on edge.

It was during an uncomfortable night that the would-be gambler awoke, groaning and muttering to himself as he got clumsily to his feet. He lurched towards the makeshift toilet, causing uneasy shuffling of dozing passengers who cursed under their breath.

The man was gone some time and Robert wondered if he'd collapsed again. He hoped he'd fall down the hole on the track below, but he was disappointed. The sliding door creaked open and the man slumped down in his seat. Soon he began to snore.

Robert tried to settle down again to sleep but his mind was in a whirl. By Steve's reckoning, every man was a potential enemy, and gradually Robert's bones and muscles ached with tension.

He was badly in need of a good stiff drink.

The train trundled its way over the rails. There were many stops at the temporary camp-sites of the men guarding the new rails, for taking on passengers and disgorging supplies for the maintenance men. They whistle-stopped at small-town stations and when they finally hit Baltimore, Robert knew that soon they would reach Washington, where his first assignment was to be.

Bill Mayfield had been most specific when he asked for information on what was happening in Washington, what the overall opinion was of these migrants going West and, more important, what was the situation concerning the Indians. Rumours were rife and it was frustrating for those in New York not to know the true situation. Should they encourage folk to go West, or should they advise caution and be dubbed fuddy-duddies by the ill-informed?

When the train finally drew up with a scream and a hissing of steam, Robert stepped down on to the station platform and felt important. There seemed to be as little danger in Washington as there was in New York. Of course there were the cut-throats in the alleyways, but Robert was used to that sort of crime. It was the unknown danger of nut-cases and painted tribesmen that made his skin crawl. What would it be like to be strung up by his thumbs and slowly roasted over a fire? The very thought made his guts rumble unpleasantly. He wished he could remain in Washington.

But the train would move on in two days. It remained in Washington just long enough to take on water for the boilers, a load of coal, food for the galley and to wait for a senator and his entourage to fill the first class coach before moving on at a leisurely pace.

Robert wondered who the high and mighty senator could be and whether he would make a good news item.

Steve Caulfield surprised him. Not once had he mentioned that he would be doing business in Washington. Now he looked down at Robert.

'You'll be all right, Robert, on your own? Don't stray too far from the city centre. I've got to visit the White House on business. You can come with me if you like, or do you want to look about you on your own?'

Robert grasped at the chance. There was no way he was going to confess that he felt intimidated by this bustling city. Pride kept him from admitting it. He pretended to consider, then he grinned,

'I might as well come along. I can always report on what it feels like to walk in the shadow of the great! By the way, d'you know who the senator is who's coming with us? And where he's heading for?'

Steve frowned as he dug into his pocket and found some change to pay the black conductor to look after their bags on board the train until their return.

'Who told you it was a senator?'

Robert shrugged.

'I guess I heard it last night when we

went for a beer.'

'Well, I wouldn't repeat that rumour if I was you, son. Just watch your mouth in future. I might not always be around to put you right on things. Now come on, I haven't time to waste. I've some papers to deliver and I want to get it over with.'

They took one of the new horse-cabs that were waiting outside the station. Robert watched eagerly as they travelled the streets and compared Washington with New York. It certainly wasn't cleaner. He missed the smell of the ocean and the wind.

Soon they stopped in front of the famous White House and Robert marvelled at its purity and size. He wandered about in the square in front of it, which was given over to grass and trees; he watched officials coming and going and counted the number of cabs which drew up and disgorged their passengers to walk up the wide pathway to the imposing entrance where two soldiers acted as guards.

Steve Caulfield's interview hadn't taken more than an hour. He came back tight-lipped and suppressing anger. He was abrupt with Robert when he asked how the interview had gone.

'None of your business!' He stalked down the path to the main gate with Robert trotting behind him.

For a while there was a strained silence as Steve stalked on in military fashion. It crossed Robert's mind that this man had known military service.

It made him wonder again about Steve and why he'd taken him under his wing. Had it been unintentional, or could it be that Steve had known who he was from the first meeting?

He could only wait and see. Meantime he could take notes of his impressions of Washington as a newcomer and send off his first telegram to Bill Mayfield. He hoped he'd be sending what his editor wanted.

They ate in a café and Steve paid the bill. It was as if he was apologizing for his rudeness. Robert ate quickly and then started to scribble down his first report.

'Where's the nearest telegraph office? Do you know,' he asked Steve when he'd finished.

'Two blocks from here,' Steve answered immediately.

'Oh, so you know Washington well then?'

'You might say that.'

'Oh!' Robert waited to see if Steve would explain further. He did not. 'Could you point me the way to it?'

'Better still, I'll come with you. I want to send a telegram myself.'

Robert soon had his report sent off. He waited for Steve, who was now scribbling down a message. He had his back to him and Robert deemed it wise not to go near him. Steve was unpredictable and he needed this man's friendship for as long as possible.

For the first time, Robert wondered just how far along the line Steve was travelling and where was he heading after that. Had he the nerve to ask him when once they got under way again? He knew Steve's attitude to questions.

But he needn't have worried. Steve brought up the subject himself when the train rumbled its way out of the station.

'The telegraph officer tells me the railway line goes well beyond Cincinnati and is moving on to St Louis. How far are you heading?'

'To the end of the line.'

'And then what?'

Robert looked a little uncertain.

'I've to buy a horse, I suppose, and bum around and make my way westward eventually. I understand if I have a horse I can take it on the railway if I ever get near one. I just have no idea what to expect.'

Robert blushed, as he remembered the pawnbroker's comments when he'd bought his gun. *Don't reckon it'll be much good against an expert, boy, but it might save your life against some petty crook!* But it was all he could afford out of Bill Mayfield's cash. He'd taken it and been too scared to death to try it out in the pawnboker's back yard.

Now he brought it out of its holster. Steve Caulfield examined it. It was an old Manhattan six-inch barrel, .31 Navy gun. He looked down the barrel and eyed its rusty interior.

'Ever used it?'

Robert blushed again and shook his head.

'Hell's bells! Bill Mayfield should be shot for sending you out West with no experience of using a gun!'

'You know Bill Mayfield?' Now Robert's jaw dropped open.

'Oh, to hell with it!' Steve said disgustedly. 'He said not to tell you. Sure, I've known Bill for years! He was once a wet behind-the-ears cub reporter like you and we tangled up and became friends. I've even wired news to him on occasion. He told me to look out for you. That you were a babe in arms and needed toughening up!' He sighed. 'I've never took to wet-nursing kids!'

Robert reared up, pride hurt.

'I don't need no looking after, mister! I'm not looking for trouble and I can fight and kick-box with the best if I have to. You don't grow up in the Bronx without knowing how to defend yourself!'

'Fighting in the Bronx is a damn sight different from fighting in the West! Most times you don't know what's hit you! There's more bushwhacking than eyeball-to-eyeball fighting, I can tell you! There's no rules and you play dirty. Understand?'

'Look, all I'm going to do is travel around and observe and write up what I've seen. As I say, I'm not looking for trouble.'

'Trouble has a nasty habit of looking for you! I know. I've stood in a bar minding my own business and drinking a beer and before I could see the bottom of the glass I was in a free-for-all and I had no idea what the rumpus was all about! If you're there, you're in it! That's the rule in the West. No one asks which side you're on. Your jaw is as good as any other to punch, and you punch back if you have any sense!'

'You make it sound like men turn into wild animals!'

'Yes, you might say that. On the other hand if you're good with a knife as well as your fists, and you tote a *real* gun, then you might just earn some real respect. Young 'uns have to earn their spurs, as they say. Older experienced fellers regard youngsters as unpredictable and dangerous. Some day, someone'll face some young guy with spirit who'll be faster on the draw than he is. Then it's curtains for him. So, until that happens, youngsters like you are prime targets!' He eyed Robert grimly, noting his reactions. He went on slowly, 'There's many a good kid, too clever for his own good, shot up and shovelled into a hole under a bush. The whole of the West is dotted with unknown graves. Remember that.'

Robert's lesson on what to expect in the West and how to combat the dangers continued as the train chugged its way along the line.

The group of passengers had changed a little. The drummer and the parson had left the train in Washington, and so had the middle-aged couple and the two schoolteachers. Two new passengers came aboard, a dark-suited man in a tall hat, carrying a black bag, who looked like a doctor, and a stout woman carrying several heavy bags. She looked pale and worn and closed her eyes as soon as she was aboard. The rest of the passengers were the same, the cowboys and their boss, the man in black, the two flashy females and the derby-hatted man who was now nursing a hangover.

All was quiet except for the hypnotic rattle of the train as it ran over its tracks. The talk ceased and both Robert and Steve closed their eyes to sleep.

Suddenly Steve was wide awake. He looked out of the window and realized the train was slowing down. He knew from experience that it should not have done so at this point. He shook Robert awake just as a great squealing of brakes and a jet of steam rent the air.

Opening a window and leaning out, Steve saw a tree trunk lying across the line. Two men on horseback, carrying drawn rifles, were waiting. Behind them in a stand of trees he glimpsed a bunch of tethered horses.

The train stopped with a sickening jerk. The two females started screaming and the stout woman opened her eyes and started to pray aloud. One of the cowboys slapped the screaming women hard and they slumped down in their seats.

Swiftly the man in black pulled one of his guns and covered Steve and Robert. He ordered one of the cowboys to open the carriage door. Then he turned his attention on Steve. Robert he ignored.

'Move a muscle and you're dead!'

Steve, in the act of reaching for his gun allowed his hands to hover in the air.

'Not my heist, mister. I ain't stopping you!' Steve smiled coolly at the gunman.

'You . . . ' pointing to the derby-hatted man, 'Get over there beside the others if you want to live.' The shaking man sidled across the coach to where Steve and Robert sat.

The gunman turned to the others.

'Right, boys, get through that door and make for the other coach. I'll be right behind you when I finish the business here!'

Steve's jaw tightned. He knew what the 'business' would be. No witnesses. The aim was to take the senator and whatever else was valuable aboard the train, and disappear until the time came for a ransom demand for the senator.

Swiftly Steve glanced at Robert who obviously hadn't guessed what the 'business' meant. He caught his eye and nodded and Robert responded. As the outlaws moved swiftly towards them to go into the next coach, Steve punched the first man while Robert kicked out at the wrist of the man in black, who was holding a gun.

The man cursed and dropped his gun. Robert followed up with a couple of quick jabs. Then Robert was being overpowered by one of the other men, but they were all of a tangle in the confined space. Robert heaved upwards, and the man on his back was flung on to those following behind.

The gunhawk scrabbled amongst the flailing arms and legs for his gun but Steve kicked it out of reach, and head-butted a cursing cowboy. The noise was horrendous. Robert managed to lift a leg and caught a man in the groin. He was flung back howling and crashed into another card-playing outlaw, landing heavily on his stomach. The man lay still while the other lay groaning and holding himself until the derby-hatted man hit him over the head with his heavy case.

Then Steve managed to get a little space around him. He drew his gun, and aimed for the man in black. His gun exploded deafeningly in the confined space. He missed and Robert saw the man pull a knife from a sheath hanging down his back, just as Steve had said it would be.

Then Robert saw the outlaw's gun on the floor. Swiftly he bent down and grasped it and, without thinking, pointed it at the man in black. He fired.

He saw the man jerk. For a moment he was still, then he reared up, the knife dropping from his hand. As a spurt of blood coloured the all-over blackness of his body, he slowly slumped to the ground.

Robert gasped and stood still, suddenly oblivious to the men lying on the floor. He was wet with sweat. This had been no fight such as he'd known back in the Bronx. Steve was right. This was for real. Those battles in the Bronx had been nothing compared to this. He staggered a little, wanting to be sick. He watched Steve with eyes that could hardly see, saw him examining bodies, leaving the dead and tying wrists together of those who were alive with their own bandannas.

'Stop gawping, boy, and help me!' rasped Steve. 'We've got to get out there and see what's going on.'

'I killed a man!' Robert gasped.

'Yes, and you'll do it again if push comes to shove! Now let's go and do some real damage!'

Robert followed him out of the coach, still dazed with reaction. Dimly he was aware of bodies lying by the tracks, while the senator's men were mopping up. He looked back at those left in the coach. The doctor who'd kept out of the fracas was now attending to the women, and the derby-hatted man was excitedly telling the tale of how he'd knocked a man out.

Suddenly, Robert's head cleared. Mercifully the raid was over and it had been foiled. There were many stories to tell. He would have to talk to all of the passengers and get their reactions. It would all make wonderful reading . . . even his own part in it. He shuddered a little, but now he could distance himself from the moment when he'd killed a man. He could write a first-hand account of what it was like to step over that invisible line and become a killer.

Steve called him again but this time he did not respond. He was too busy scribbling notes in his little book.

3

High up on the mountain range, Jake Falco crouched on a ridge looking through his glasses at the scene below. The standing train looked like a child's toy. He watched the tiny moving figures that from this distance looked like ants, scurrying around the train. He frowned. Something had gone wrong!

He swung round to glare at the three men behind him, his lieutenants, men he thought he could trust.

'They knew! They were ready for us! Goddammit! If it hadn't been for the wound in my hand, I should have been with them! Now,' he studied the three coldly, 'which one of you sold us out?'

He saw the flicker of fear come and go on the youngest member of the three. He remembered the thrashing he'd given the kid a couple of months ago for getting rip-roaring drunk after a raid and opening his mouth too wide. The mangy piece of shit had tried getting his own back!

Quick as a flash his left hand snaked out, his right hand useless, and grabbed his second gun. The kid dropped with a neat bullet between the eyes. The other two men stood aghast.

'Get rid of him! Throw him in a gully and give the coyotes a feast!' He turned back to watch what was going on down below.

Then, as the two men carried the kid away, he caught his breath, for he'd recognized the big man down below. He knew that walk, the set of the broad shoulders. If he would just turn his head . . .

It was as if he'd ordered the man to do so, for Steve Caulfield suddenly turned and looked towards the mountain range.

Jake Falco swore. He thought he'd sent Caulfield to hell back in the Sierra Nevada. The bastard had the luck of the devil and he sure got around! It was as if Caulfield was riding herd on him and his men!

Falco flexed his right hand. It was still too stiff to risk a fast draw face to face. Oh, he could use his left hand for shooting, but he hadn't the speed necessary to take on a professional gunhawk as he knew Steve Caulfield to be.

He started to sweat and it was fear not the sun that brought out the beads of perspiration. Quickly he turned away and made for the tethered horses. There was no use in thinking that any of his men, not even the gunman, Charley Knox, who'd taken his place as leader would have got away. Now his gang, which had been so numerous was reduced to the three of them.

Steve Caulfield had a lot to answer for. He'd get the son of a bitch, if it took a lifetime.

His mind was busy, working out ways of revenge, as the three men picked their way down the steep hillside. So, the rumour that that train was carrying the railroad workers' payroll, had been just that. A rumour put out to tempt him and he'd been cocky enough to fall for it!

The more he thought about it the angrier he became! The men with him were silent. They knew Falco enough to know that he could explode into violence at any time; killing the kid had shown them just how dangerous he was at this time. They looked at each other and knew that each had the same thought. Either of them could have shot him in the back but held off because they needed his brains and nerve. They'd never been so successful in their long careers of bank-robbing and train hold-ups on their own. He had been the one who plotted their raids and until now, they'd had cash to burn, liquor and women galore and an easy carousing life until the next raid. Now it had all gone wrong.

If they killed Falco, they would be back to petty thieving and the high life would be a thing of the past.

They were down the mountain slope before Pete ventured a question.

'What we do now boss?'

Falco gave him a vicious look. 'Get back to the hideout. What else?'

'I thought — '

'Shut up! You're not paid to think! I do the thinking, and we go back to the hideout. Is that clear?'

Pete nodded and Frank kept silent. There didn't seem to be anything he could say. They followed the trail and kept clear of any small hamlets they passed on the way, even though their throats were dry and their guts stuck to their backbones. There would be no roistering today.

★   ★   ★

Steve Caulfield strode to where the senator stood waiting and stretched out his hand. They clasped hands and John S Witham put an arm around Steve and hugged him.

'It paid off, Steve! The bastards fell

53

for it! By God, I was sweating! I'm not up to this lark, believe me! I don't know how you had the nerve to sit in that coach knowing you were amongst that gang of cut-throats!'

Steve Caulfhield smiled.

'I kept cool by talking to a kid reporter. It eased the tension, but I was worried about the women-folk.'

'Yes, it was a pity we couldn't have kept the women out of it but, apart from being frightened, they're none the worse.' Then he hesitated. 'Steve, we haven't found Falco. He isn't among the dead.' He gave Steve a long considering look, watching for his reaction.

Steve felt a gut disappointment.

'The son of a bitch is a wily bastard!' he growled. 'Did anyone get away?'

'Not a single one, Steve. My boys were on them before they knew what had hit them. I reckon he's on his own now.'

'You sure about none getting away?'

'I briefed my men to watch out for

runners. None was reported and by the count, we've got upwards of fifteen bodies. The number who we reckoned got away in the Sierra Nevada raid.'

'Well, if he's alone and on the run, he'll be as dangerous as a mountain cat and just as unpredictable. The only recourse is to keep after him and give him no chance to recruit any new members.'

'I was hoping you would say that, Steve. The department wants you to keep under cover whatever the outcome of this sortie.'

Steve Caulfield turned and surveyed the mountain range. He gave a rueful grin.

'It'll be like looking for a needle in a haystack, hunting that range for one man! I suppose it can be done.'

'Come on now, Steve, you've taken on worse assignments than looking for Falco!'

'Yes, but I've had contacts and back-up when I wanted it. Out there, the terrain's new to me.'

'Well, take that kid with you! He can always watch your back if nothing else and it'll give the kid something real to write about.' He laughed, thinking of Steve toting a junior kid with him.

Steve looked surprised and then said thoughtfully,

'Maybe it isn't such a bad idea at that. The kid's green but smart. His reflexes were good and he didn't lose his head. It can't be less dangerous for him trailing after me than being left on his own. At least he'd get some mighty exciting material to send back to Bill Mayfield.'

John S Witham raised his eyebrows.

'So the kid works for the *Tribune*? He must be smart or Bill wouldn't have sent him West. I think he should tag along with you. If the kid reports the run-up to your catching the most ruthless outlaw in recent years, his reputation will be made. You'll be doing the boy a favour!'

★   ★   ★

Robert Malkovitch opened his eyes wide when the offer was made.

'You mean to tell me you *knew* those fellers were outlaws?' Steve smiled at the wonder and surprise the kid showed.

'Jesus! I would have messed myself if I'd known! So you're working for the government as well as the railroad? You're not pulling my leg, are you?'

'Look, son, I'm not in the habit of pulling legs. This is serious stuff, those bodies out there bear me out. Do you want to come with me and help catch Falco, or not? It will be dangerous, but you'll learn how to defend yourself in the West. I'll be teaching you things a kid like you would never learn on your own. Besides, think of the stories that you'll be able to send back East!'

That settled it. By God, he could become more famous than that Buntline feller who wrote those dime novels all about the fictional West! This was the opportunity of a lifetime! Those reporters back home who had jeered at his flights of fancy would have to eat their words! His eyes shone.

'Well? What d'you think, or are you just a kid with a yellow streak down your back?'

He straightened angrily.

'I got no yellow streak, mister! I'll come with you and I'll sure show you that I'm not hanging on your coat-tails!'

'Good. That's what I like to hear. You've got a lot to learn. You can get rid of that thing you call a gun. I'll see you get a proper shooter, compliments of the government, and a rifle to boot!'

'Hey now, that sounds too good to be true. What about a horse?'

'You can take your pick.' He nodded to the stand of trees where several horses were tethered. 'They'll all be fast and good stayers. We'll both want two horses, one to ride and the other as a pack-horse. Come on, I'll give you a lesson in horseflesh.'

Heart beating rapidly, for Robert wasn't going to admit he didn't know one end of a horse from the other, he followed in Steve's footsteps until they came to the row of animals. He watched while Steve ran a practised hand over rumps and down legs and lifted hoofs to inspect horseshoes.

Robert stepped back a little as the horses snorted and tossed their heads. He watched how Steve calmed them with strokes and softly spoken words.

His guts knotted when the chestnut Steve was handling reared its head and snorted, dancing a little in response to the strange scent of this stranger. Steve saw the apprehensive look on Robert's face.

'It's all right, son. She's just taking my measure. It's when a horse flattens its ears and rolls back his eyes that you've got to look out. Now, let's have you up in the saddle and I'll give you a rough idea of how to take control of the beast. You say you've never been aboard a horse before?'

'No sir! Never had no call to ride in New York!'

Steve grunted, and shook his head.

'Bill Mayfield knows as little as you do about the West if he thought you could ride the rails wherever you want to go.'

'He *did* say I could buy a horse!'

Steve grunted again.

'Easy to say, boy. I'd like to get the bastard here and give *him* a lesson or two! I'd make his ass blister!'

Robert took a deep breath.

'You don't mean that, do you? I mean about the blisters?'

Steve laughed.

'Son, you're not a real rider until you've got corns on your ass and on your thighs! Now let's get down to it. Up you get and grip her belly with your knees.' Robert put a foot in the heavy iron stirrup and, as the mare danced away from him, strove to heave himself across her broad back. It felt as if he was being split in half when he finally rolled into the saddle.

He clung to the pommel, a sweaty leathery smell assailing his nose along with the sweat from the mare.

It seemed a hell of a way from the ground.

Dimly he was conscious of Steve shoving the reins into his hand. The other hand still clung to the pommel.

'Now boy, pull on the reins and feel the bit in her mouth. No jerks or sawing at the bit or she'll cause a rumpus. Pull on the left or right side to turn. Pull both together to stop. Now, you trot her round and round and make a figure of eight and feel the control you have over her.'

'How do I get her to trot?' gasped Robert. He was hot and sweaty and he knew it was fear.

'Kick her in the ribs, is all.'

Robert, nervous and unsure, kicked her hard. She at once leapt into a gallop, taking great strides. The wind whistled in Robert's face. He forgot about the bridle reins and clung to the pommel, thinking that that was what it was for.

Then the mare turned suddenly to

avoid a tree trunk. She skipped a little and Robert sailed over her head. The ground came up fast and he rolled and lay still, stunned but aware of the mare's hoofs pounding the dust close by.

He heard Steve's bellowing laughter, and it turned his fear into a steely resolve. He'd learn to ride if it killed him. He wanted Steve's respect, not his mockery because he was a city kid.

He did not realize that Steve already admired this kid from the Bronx for taking on this nearly impossible assignment.

Robert sat up, shaking his head. He'd once felt this way when Roughhouse Baker had picked him up and twirled him around in Molly's bar and thrown him to the ground. This dirt was as hard as Molly's saloon's planked floor and he'd survived that all right.

Now he staggered to his feet and watched Steve stalk the mare which was now grazing on a tuft of coarse grass. He was speaking softly to her. The mare's ears were pricked but she eyed Steve with curiosity. She snuffled rather than snorted as Steve moved closer.

'All right, old girl,' Steve said softly, 'it wasn't your fault he kicked you to a gallop. That's what you're trained for. That's my girl! Come on now.' Suddenly Steve reached into his pocket and pulled out a piece of raw sugar. 'Come and get it.'

Robert saw with surprise that the head came down in meek acceptance, the nose caressed Steve's hand, the sugar disappeared between her jaws and Steve was firmly holding the bridle.

'It just takes patience and bribery. This here animal has been well treated by her owner. A horse can be a man's best friend if treated right. He can save a man's life if he's good at his job. Now up you get again and this time just a gentle nudge and she'll know what to do.'

This time, Robert hauled himself aboard feeling easier but rather stiff. The bruises would come later. A gentle nudge as Steve recommended and they were off. As Steve stood and watched, Robert remembered to guide her into a figure of eight and soon he was relaxing and quite enjoying the sensation of being carried along upon a moving body.

'Go with the mare. Lift when she lifts. Use your feet. Feel the stirrups and lift your ass. There now, you don't look so much like a monkey on a stick!'

Robert gave Steve a grin as he obeyed his instructions. It wasn't so bad after all.

'Now try a canter, kid. A little more nudge, a bit more pressure this time. That's right. Do another figure of eight and let's see how you control her.'

Fearfully, Robert gave her a slight kick with both feet near her underbelly and she took off at a gentle speed.

His heart swelled with pride. Jesus! He could really enjoy this way of travelling. No wonder cowboys sang songs about their horses! If this mare and he could really get to know each other, he reckoned he would get real fond of her. His face beamed.

When they came round again, Steve saw the pleasure in Robert's eyes and was satisfied. The kid would soon get broken in. What he had to learn now was to fall easy and to use his own wit when unusual circumstances cropped up, like riding herd or charging another horse while watching some bastard who wanted to shoot his head off.

But that would all come later. No need to fill the boy with foreboding at this stage.

'So, you're satisfied with the chestnut? You could try another if you want.'

Robert shook his head, running his hand down her neck and patting it. 'I like her. I think we'll get along just fine.'

'Good. Now I'll pick me a horse and a couple as pack-horses. The rest will be taken by the senator's men.'

'What do we do now, Steve?'

'Cast around and see if we can find some new hoofprints. The senator's men will fan out and take a look.

They're all good hunters. We'll eat and be ready if we get results.' He smiled grimly. 'We let the men do the work. We save ourselves for the hunt. We've a long way to go and we must save our strength. Now you can get back to the train and organize those cooks to rustle us up some grub, while I catch me some horses!'

4

Steve Caulfield, with Robert riding close behind, followed the tracker who'd located the suspect hoofprints. They drew up beside the man, who now leaned across his horse's neck and peered at the broken ground and disturbed stones.

'I reckon those varmints left their horses here. See, the grass is newly nibbled. The tracks lead up to the top of that butte yonder.' He pointed to a faint track that might have been a goat-track but wasn't. Robert marvelled at the man's keen eyesight and envied his expertise at reading sign.

'Did you climb to the top?' asked Steve abruptly.

The man shrugged. 'No need to, boss. It's as plain as the nose on your face. Falco and at least three others climbed up and took a look at what was happening below. I reckon the trail will be picked up south or south-west of here.'

'Nevertheless, we're going to check it out, mister. You could be wrong.'

The man's face darkened. He drew himself up.

'I'm not paid to be wrong! But go ahead. I'll report back to my boss!' He wheeled his horse around and took off at a smart lick back to the train. Steve looked after him thoughtfully.

'There goes a man with ruffled feelings.'

Robert looked at him curiously.

'Why did you doubt him, Steve?'

Steve rubbed his bristly chin. 'I reckon he was a bit too slick in finding these tracks. Maybe he got lucky. Maybe he didn't. Falco pays well for information. It isn't the first time he's infiltrated government agents.'

'You mean that man could be one of them?' Robert gasped, wide-eyed.

'You never want to take strangers at face value, boy. Everybody has an axe to grind. Now, we'll just take a look-see. If I'm wrong about that man, I'll apologize to him in my mind.' He grinned, swung a leg and dropped to the ground like some graceful cat. Robert followed more slowly; his whole body ached.

They climbed the steep escarpment while the horses took advantage of the sparse scrub grass. Robert's heart thumped at the unaccustomed exercise while Steve, agile as the said cat, arrived at the ridge well in front of Robert. He was already moving along the ridge looking for sign and soon found it. He knelt and made out four sets of footprints. Then he stood up and surveyed the valley below and the standing train. The men down below looked like dots. He took off his hat and wiped his forehead with his bandanna.

'Huh!' he grunted as Robert joined him. 'It looks as if that feller was right after all. Look, you can see where they hunkered down and watched. One of them even smoked a cigarette.' He pointed to a stub. It looked very fresh.

'So that tracker was right,' murmured Robert. His eyes took in the scene and tried to differentiate between the various patterns of the boot-impressions. Then he frowned. Surely that was blood on that stone where the ants were collecting in a kind of frenzy?

He caught Steve's arm.

'Hey! Isn't that blood down there?' He knelt to have a closer look.

Steve hunkered down beside him and his face was grave.

'Yes, that's blood. Now I wonder what happened here.' He took a closer look about him, his eyes narrowing as he saw drag marks leading away to a fissure in the rocky ground.

Taking care to follow the trail, he came to a stop beside the edge of the crevasse. Narrowing his eyes to pierce the gloom far down below, he seemed to see a bundle of old clothes. He swore under his breath.

'What is it?' Robert asked, suddenly breathless. This was real. He had a queer feeling running up and down his spine, that they were to find something gruesome . . .

Steve did not answer but swung his legs over the edge and slowly climbed down to where he could see what the bundle was. However, the whiff coming from below prepared him for what he would find.

He turned the body over. Already it was being invaded by ants. He took one look at the gunshot wound, then climbed out of the fissure and looked at Robert grimly.

'I reckon Falco is another man short. It looks as if we're hunting just three men and he'll be dangerous, like a cornered beast. We'll get back, get the pack-horses and be on our way!'

Robert got out his notebook and stub of pencil to write some notes as a bid for normality. His fingers trembled.

'No time for that, kid. You'll have to do your writing when we bed down for the night! Let's get going!'

★ ★ ★

Jake Falco cursed as they rode over the arid broken country. Huge rocks reared up amidst the scrubland. There were no headlong gallops. They had to pick their way carefully for fear of lamed fetlocks. The sun beat down on bowed shoulders and even through the thick flannel shirts it felt like molten metal. Sweat darkened the fabric which clung to their perspiring bodies like a second skin.

Falco badly needed a drink. He could feel his tongue starting to swell.

'We've got to find water soon,' he croaked. 'Let the horses pick their own way. They'll smell water before we do.'

They all relaxed their hold on the reins and pulled their hats well over their eyes to try and keep out the burning heat.

They were lucky. They found not only a spring of glutinous mud but a soddy partly built into a hillside. Normally they would have ridden past it and never known it was there, but the horses whinnied and lengthened their stride.

There was no one at home when they burst in through the door. It was a one-room shack with no window. It was dark and smelled damp along with the scent of unwashed body and badly cured animal skins.

They ransacked the place, looking for both water and food. They found only chilli beans and a scraping of mouldy flour in a wooden barrel.

Falco cursed. He knelt by the stone fireplace and felt the grey ash. It was cold. The fire had not been lit for days. He cursed again and looked about him. There was nothing of value. The place was stripped clean of any evidence that someone had lived there.

'Frank, look around and see if you can find something to carry water in. Get down to that puddle and dig down. See what you can get. We'll have to have water.'

'Right, boss.'

The younger of the two men went

outside, glad to get away from Falco who was sure working himself up into a frenzy. He'd take his time. Pete was best at keeping Falco from going off at half-cock.

His guts rumbled. Maybe it would calm Falco somewhat if he hunted for dry wood for a fire, and if he could come up with some half-decent water they could cook up some of them there beans. They would be better than nothing.

Inside the soddy, Falco glared at Pete.

'We're in a fix, Pete. That bastard'll not let up on us! We need to eat and rest. Those horses will give out if we're not careful and I don't intend walking through that wasteland!'

'How about doubling back and ambushing him? He'll not expect us to be waiting for him.'

'He's too fly for that. Besides, there's not enough cover. He'll be trigger-happy and by God, he's got eyes in his ass! No, we'll make for the mountain range and away from the railtrack.'

'What about the Indians and the altitude? There's snow up there and we're not dressed for blinding snow-storms.'

Falco turned on him viciously.

'Right! What do you suggest? You seem to be the smartass.'

Pete looked at him sullenly.

'I say we should ambush him!'

'OK! You go right ahead and do it and if you kill him, I'll give you an extra share in the stash we have!'

Pete straightened up, eyes agleam.

'You mean that, boss? If I kill him, I get an extra share?'

'I said it, didn't I? It would be worth it if that bastard was dead!'

Pete looked at the door. He didn't want Frank overhearing the conversation.

'Look, I'll go back the way we came and wait for him but don't tell Frank. I'm not sharing with him or anybody else!'

'Spoken like a true mercenary!' Falco

spoke mockingly.

'We got a deal?'

'Yes. You put your life on the line, kill that son of a bitch and I'll be grateful. You won't lose out. When Falco makes a deal, he keeps his word!'

Just then, there came the crack of a rifle shot and Falco sprang to the door, left hand on his gun, with Pete at his shoulder.

They stared ahead but nothing moved. Cautiously Falco stepped outside and took a look around. Where in hell was Frank? Then he spotted him in a crumpled heap by the muddy spring. He was just starting forward when another rifle shot slammed into the rough pine planks that made up the front wall of the soddy.

He jumped back, knocking Pete who was just behind him, and slammed the door.

'Who in hell's out there?' Pete rasped.

'I don't know but he's got one of those new long-distance Spencer rifles, and he means business!'

'Jesus! We're trapped in here!' Pete began to panic.

Falco slapped his face hard.

'Get hold of yourself! We're two to his one. Take a look at the planks at that side of the door and if one's loose, pull it out. I'll do the same on this side. We don't have the back side to worry about as it's dug into the hillside. If we stay quiet, he'll come and we'll get him when he shows himself.'

Falco began to pull at the ancient half-rotten planks. One splintered and he pulled and kicked with maniacal strength until he had a six-inch gap freed, enough to shoot through if whoever was out there made a sudden sortie.

Out of the corner of his eye he saw that Pete had done likewise. Now they had two chances to shoot whoever was stalking them.

They heard a shrill whistle. What in hell..? Falco tried to get a broad view of what was going on. Then he swore as three wild dogs that looked like cross-bred wolves charged up to the soddy with mouths open, fangs dripping spittle and howling enough to chill the marrow in their bones.

They hurled themselves against the flimsy door, which seemed to shudder. Falco sprang to it and slipped a plank of wood in the crude wooden hooks to hold it in place.

Pete was desperately trying to get a bead on one of the leaping animals but they moved too quickly for him. He was trembling and it took him all his time to hold his gun steady.

Falco risked a quick shot which missed and set the dogs to more frenzied attacks on the door. There was only one thing to do. Open the door and blast the dogs as they sprang inside. Fleetingly he wondered whether Pete would be up to it. Pete's face was ashen.

'I'm going to open the door,' Falco yelled. 'Be ready and fire at the bastards!'

'No!' screamed Pete, but Falco was already pulling away the plank and the door opened with a sickening jerk.

The dogs, surprised, hesitated and then leapt forward as Falco fired. He dropped one, then turned his gun on the other. Pete, still trembling, fired two shots but missed. The leader sprang at his throat with a deep growling sound. Falco fired and saw the back of the beast's head blown off, but it was too late. The fangs were buried deep into Pete's jugular and blood spouted from him like a fountain.

Then Falco knew real fear, for the third dog leapt at him with a ferocious snarling and Falco's gun clicked on to an empty barrel.

He kicked out and caught the slavering jaws a mighty swipe which hunched the dog in his tracks. He yelped and shook his head but it didn't stop him.

Then a huge figure darkened the doorway and a deep voice boomed out to stay the stunned beast. At once, the animal slunk down on to his belly, his growl now a whine in his throat. His eyes were bright and unyielding on Falco. He was ready to spring at any time.

Falco drew breath and looked up at the man in the doorway. Christ! He was tall! More like a bear than a man, what with the long shaggy hair and beard. Falco sucked in his breath. What would happen now? The son of a bitch could throttle him with one hand, and here he was with an empty gun!

He stood while the man looked him up and down, the rifle pointing menacingly at Falco's gut.

'I've got two dogs dead because of you,' the booming voice said menacingly. 'I should put a bullet in you right now but that would be too good for you. I think I should have a little amusement out of you before . . . '

He stopped abruptly and listened to a faint howl in the far distance. 'That's Tommy, looking to get his end away.' He laughed, and Falco, looking into the man's eyes, thought incredulously: the son of a bitch is mad! He's talking as if those cursed animals are folks! He swallowed. What did he mean by a little amusement?

He soon knew.

The hunter, for Falco reckoned such he must be, by the smell of badly cured skins that hung about him, suddenly lunged forward. He moved swiftly for so big a man and before Falco knew his intent, he had an arm across his throat and clamped around his neck. Choking, Falco tried to fight free. He kicked out blindly and caught his captor on the leg but he was as impervious to pain as if he, Falco, was an irritating flea. Then heaving him upright into the air he carried him outside. Falco was tied with a rawhide rope to the wheel of a broken-down wagon.

No matter how he struggled, he was like a baby in arms.

'Now we'll see just how long you can stand the sun and the flies. Three days and you can go free! What about that, eh? I'm a kindly man and I don't like killing! You stick it out for three days and you can walk out of here!' The booming laugh came. 'There'll be no horse for you. If you're tough enough to withstand three days then you're tough enough to get out on foot!'

'You're crazy!' gasped Falco. 'You're goddam crazy! Better to kill me now and get it over with! Hell! I wouldn't treat a dog this way!'

'Neither would I. Dogs are my friends. They're loyal and don't turn on and betray a man. I've took years to train these dogs and you and that bastard over there killed two of them in minutes. I don't take kindly to anyone hurting any of my pack.'

'Pack? How many more have you got?'

'You'll find out if you survive the next three days.' With a laugh, the hunter walked away. Falco watched him drag Pete's body out of the soddy and dump it on what looked like a refuse tip.

Falco licked dry lips. Already the sun

was getting at him and sweating out what moisture there was in his body. A great anger swelled in him. He'd be damned if he would go off his head and die! He'd show that son of a bitch what an ex-army officer could live through. He'd been in some tight corners before and come out of them. He sure as hell wasn't going to provide amusement and pleasure for this maniac.

He tried wriggling his hands in an attempt to loosen the knots. If he could only get one hand free . . .

But that scumsucker knew how to tie knots, and Falco was only perspiring all the more in his efforts. So he closed his eyes, bent his head, tried to relax and waited . . . and waited, until, when night came, he fell into an uneasy oblivion.

The night grew colder. Falco woke with a start and tried to move. But now his muscles had swelled and stiffened. He stifled a groan and then became aware of the big man squatting beside him. The stinking dog's turd was eating stew from a dirty bowl and the steam of it was wafting under Falco's nose. His guts rumbled.

Then the big man poured water from a bucket into a mug, slopping water on to the ground. Falco closed his eyes as his stomach knotted.

The bearlike man laughed.

'The water's a bit brackish but it's filtered. Takes almost a day to get a bucketful. No more water around these parts for a day's ride. Thought I'd let you know.'

'Bastard!' The word came out hoarsely through dry swollen lips, but the big man only chuckled and walked away.

Dimly Falco was aware of moonlight and then he sank again into a nightmarish void. A strong voice in his head drew him back from the black pit. It said over and over again: *You're an officer in the Fifth Cavalry and the motto is* Fight until Death. *You're an officer* . . . The words went on and on growing louder until he awakened.

His tongue stuck to the top of his mouth, a dry swollen thing that tasted of bile and decay. There was no more twisting of his guts. He was beyond feeling. His head hung down and when he forced his eyes open, he could see tiny ants going about their business. He saw with surprise that he'd pissed himself and shat, and the ants were having a field day. His eyes closed again and he was only aware of his own stink.

A rough hand grabbed his hair and pulled back his head. He half opened a bleary eye to see the bushy-bearded man staring down at him. He tried to speak but his mouth wouldn't obey him. Yet the strong voice inside him kept repeating the motto: *Fight until Death!*

The man spat in disgust. There was no amusement to be had in watching an unconscious victim. He reckoned the feller was three-parts dead. He might as well cut him down and throw him into the crevasse where he dumped his animal bones.

Falco was dimly aware that his hands were freed, that the tension had gone from his arm muscles, and he was being slung over a broad back. A little later, he was flying through the air and landing smack amongst a stinking rancid pile of rubbish with a jolt that brought him wideawake.

He lay still until he was sure he was alone. Then slowly and painfully he raised himself upright on one elbow. It was then that he realized he was lying uncomfortably on a criss-cross mass of bones and rotting flesh.

The pit was alive too. He heard the scurryings of small rodents and felt the bite of an invasion of fleas which attacked him hungrily.

Jesus! he mouthed and tried weakly to climb out of the pit.

It was past noon when he finally rolled out on to the ground. He lay panting, the world around him spinning madly. Then he rolled into a mesquite bush, a relief from the pitiless sun.

He remembered what an old Indian

had told him about cactus plants and, despite bloody hands from the spines, he tore a juicy pad and sucked on it greedily. Never had moisture tasted so good. His head was clearing rapidly. He was conscious of sun blisters on his forehead and around his eyes. Sweat stung and the pain sharpened his brain. *Fight until Death* . . .

All was quiet. He would make his way to that muddy pool. He bellied slowly and patiently towards it. Then he saw that the big man was lying on his back, snoring, the remains of a meal beside him, a half-empty coffee-pot and an empty whiskey bottle near by.

Falco showed his teeth in a fierce grin. This was one time he was going to enjoy himself!

Quietly he picked up the discarded knife the man had been using. Just as he was about to strike, he heard a growl. The remaining wolfdog, who'd been lying in the shade, leapt at him. At once the big man was awake and reaching for his gun.

Falco lashed out with the knife as the beast sprang at him stabbing its chest, but not before the strong jaws clamped on his injured arm and tore at the flesh.

The big man hesitated, gun in hand. The great beast was shielding Falco's body. It all happened in the time it took to draw breath. Two shots rang out in quick succession and Falco found himself lying under a bloodied dog. He wondered vaguely what had happened, but the pain in his arm was excruciating. He groaned and lay still, the warm body of the dog covering him.

Then it was kicked aside and he was staring up at a stranger, a mountain man by his dress.

'Who're you?' Falco asked weakly.

The stranger looked down at him, stony-eyed.

'I might ask who you are, but I'm not going to, because it looks mighty like you're no friend of the wolfman here.' He came and squatted down by the big man who lay on his back, his eyes wide open, staring a dead man's stare. 'I've been after this son of a bitch for months! He's been robbing my traps.'

He stood up and looked about him, evidently satisfied with what he saw. 'So there's been a fight. I won't ask you what about but I see those cursed wolfhounds of his are dead. For that I thank you.' Without any further ado he was gone, trotting out of sight amongst the cacti and the scrub.

'Hey! Wait a minute!' But the man was gone.

Falco cursed and tried to sit up to stanch the blood. He crawled over to the wolfman and tore at his shirt. Slowly and painfully he bandaged his gaping wound, knowing full well it should have been cleaned and disinfected with a slug of whiskey poured over it. He was exhausted with the effort and lay still until he could gather enough strength to crawl to the soddy. If he was to live, he must hide out in this noisome place until such time as he could fork a horse again and ride.

He thought of the tethered horses.

They would need pasture and water but no determination on his part could make him look to them at this time. He needed rest.

Inside the soddy he found fresh food and half a bucket of brackish water. He drank sparingly again. He knew the danger of drinking heartily when dehydrated. He would eat later but now, head swimming, he collapsed on the big man's stinking bed.

5

Robert's spine ached and his behind was a mass of bruises. The inside of his knees were red-raw but he gritted his teeth. He would no more let on to Steve Caulfield about his condition than he would confess about his first disastrous experience with Amy Spengler in the back alley behind Mr Spengler's grocery store.

He hardly noticed his surroundings. He was aware of the heat and flies but he followed Steve doggedly. How Steve seemed to know his way through this cursed wilderness was an eye-opener to him.

He reckoned they were following Falco's trail, but even though Steve pointed out sign to him, he was too immersed in his own troubles to take any real notice.

Steve drew rein and turned in the

saddle to watch the boy trailing behind. He noted the drooping head, the stiffly held body and he was hard put not to grin. He knew what the kid was going through. He'd gone through it himself many years ago; too many, he thought grimly.

But the kid would harden up. All the tenderfoots did. It was only a matter of time. One thing was sure, this kid was a fighter. He'd make a good Westerner if he lived long enough.

Now he frowned and cursed Bill Mayfield for sending such a babe in arms to report on what was going on in the West these days. Someday there would be a reckoning and if he came face to face with Mayfield again, he'd punch him on the jaw . . .

'We'll camp here,' he said abruptly. He alighted from his horse and led it and his pack-horse to two thin larches. He roped the two horses to the trees with a rawhide lariat.

'Come on, and I'll show you how to tether your horses to this rope and the knot to use,' he said to Robert.

Robert slid stiffly to the ground, every bone shrieking in protest. He grabbed the bridle of his mount and the long rein of his pack-horse and followed slowly. He tried the knot Steve carefully showed him — a loop which could be pulled loose in an emergency. It took his mind off himself. When he felt efficient, he left the two horses in a row with Steve's and then found that Steve was already gathering large flat stones to build an Indian-type fire.

Steve rose from his knees and picked the biggest ant off his pants that Robert had ever seen. It was as big as some of the cockroaches back home.

'Jesus! Just look at that!'

'That's nothing to what you'll come up against. Everything is larger than life out West,' Steve replied evenly. 'Now, as to this fire. I'm showing you the Indian way if you want to cook on hot stones. The stones can be built up higher, like a little wall and then the fire's kept low and at night it won't be seen. Get it? If you want a fire at night you must remember the human predators as well as the wild animals. Even now we're being watched!'

'You're funning, aren't you?' Robert looked uneasily around.

Steve laughed.

'It's all right, kid. You're not going to get an arrow in the ribs. Most of the Powhatan tribes and the Chickahominy are friendly. Kept that way by Washington bribes, I might add. They're useful. Know every inch of ground and can foretell the weather days ahead. I've got some good friends amongst the Indians.'

'I thought they were all savages! I've heard tales . . . '

'Not savages, son. Just folk with a different outlook from ours. How would you like it if some strangers came from a far country and took your homeland by force?'

'Hmm, I never thought of it like that.'

'Well, think, boy. If you're going to be a success out West you should learn how other folk think and reason and learn what's an insult and always respect the red man. Of course there are those who remember old hatreds. How the white men broke promises in the past. Some don't trust us any more. They are the wild and free peoples, those not confined to the reservations. Those are the ones you've got to watch.'

Robert swallowed.

'I don't think I'll be meeting many of them!'

'You never know, kid, you never know! Now, we'll gather some dry wood and have us a good fire. It's a good place this. We're in a kind of basin and we won't be attracting any large animals.' He glanced slyly at Robert and then said softly with meaning, 'Not unless we happen to be camping beside a mountain cat's lair!' Robert jumped nervously and Steve grinned. 'Don't fret yourself. There's no sign of a wild animal living close by.'

'How d'you know?'

'No droppings, no scraping of claws against the trees, no sign of old bones lying around and not a sign of cubs or tufts of hair caught up on lowhanging branches of bushes, and no smell.'

'You saw all that as we were riding by?' Robert marvelled at Steve. His eyes must have been darting here and there and seeing things Robert didn't know existed.

'Look, I've ranged all over the West since I was knee-high to a coyote. For me, this land is a book and I'm reading it all the time. You, now, see what you see and put it down in words in that little book of yours. Me, I stow it all away up here.' He pointed to his head. 'Now, let's not waste time. Go and find a bundle of dry wood and I'll get out the makings for our supper.'

When Robert returned with an armful of wood, Steve had taken bedrolls from the pack-horses and there was a bundle waiting to be opened by the stones that were to be the fireplace.

Quickly Steve showed Robert how to

start the fire with dry lichen and grass and then to build small thin sticks in a kind of tepee style. Then he used his tinderbox. As Robert watched the smoke from the tinderbox turn to flame, he let out his breath. So that was how it was done. The flames leapt up and now Steve said with a smile,

'You can take over now. Add some small branches at first and get them well alight and then you can pile up the bigger stuff while I go and see if I can find water.'

Robert looked nervously around when he was alone. He remembered Steve's observation about being watched and wondered whether there was someone hiding up on the ridge looking down at his amateurish efforts to keep the fire going. But there was no movement, only the faint stirring of the low scrub trees. Steve was gone for quite a long time. The fire was roaring away and already red embers were forming. Robert opened the bundle and pulled out a black frying pan, a coffeepot and two tin mugs. There was also a bag of coffee which smelled good, and a sack of flour.

He was just beginning to get anxious about Steve when he returned. He was carrying a jackrabbit in one hand and a hat dripping with water in the other. He came striding into camp with a jaunty spring in his step. He threw down the rabbit and carefully poured the water from his hat into the coffee-pot.

'We're in luck! Caught the jackrabbit on the hop and there's a small stream not too far away. I came on it by chance. I saw muddy footprints and knew there must be a drinking-hole for the animals somewhere near. I followed the tracks and there it was! We'll eat well tonight. Now, can you make panbread?'

Robert shook his head.

'Never had to. Always got bread from the baker.' He grinned. 'Mostly pinched when the baker wasn't looking!'

Steve laughed.

'A survivor, just like me. Now, if ever

I had to live in a big city, I'd have you with me to show me the ropes!'

Suddenly Robert felt better. Steve had said they were both survivors. It was just that Robert was clean out of his own environment. He didn't feel such an incompetent fool any longer.

'Right!' he said enthusiastically. 'What can I do to help?'

'You can skin that rabbit while I make the panbread. Cut it up into small pieces and we'll roast the bits over the fire. It'll taste better than rattlesnake!'

Robert's eyes bulged as he looked at the jackrabbit and his stomach heaved at the thought of eating rattlesnake. Slowly he picked up the stiffening carcass.

'Where do I start?'

'Slit its belly and turn out its guts,' Steve said casually, 'and then peel back the skin over its back legs and pull the skin right back to the head. Like pulling the skin off a snake!'

Robert's hand was covered in blood at the first nervous plunge of the knife and he closed his eyes as the hot blood and guts tumbled out on to the ground.

Steve watched him out of the corner of his eye as Robert went to work on the skin. He concluded the skin wouldn't be worth curing because of the way Robert was handling it. But the kid was learning.

Much later, Robert sat back, replete. He licked his fingers. The jackrabbit had been good, despite the disgusting way he'd prepared it for cooking. The panbread had been delicious and there was enough left over for tomorrow's breakfast. Now he felt drowsy. All he wanted to do was sleep.

Then he jerked into full consciousness when Steve said calmly,

'You take first watch. Wake me when the moon is high in the sky looking down at us from between those trees over there.'

'How long will that be?'

'Oh, I guess three . . . four hours. Why?'

Robert shrugged.

'Just wondering. What should I do?'

'Keep the fire burning. Look at that rifle of yours and see how it works. Tomorrow, I'll give you a lesson in shooting before we move on, and, Malko . . . '

'Yes?'

'Keep awake. Our lives might depend on it!'

The night dragged and Robert walked about to keep alert. He walked over to the horses, but they too were sleeping and he decided not to disturb them. His own mare twitched an ear but that was all. He viewed her with mixed feelings. She was the cause of his sore behind.

Then at last the moon shone high through the trees. He touched Steve's shoulder. Steve was instantly awake and reaching for his gun. He laughed when he saw Robert's amazement.

'Sorry, kid, it's a reaction I get when I'm touched. You'll get used to me in time.'

Robert lay down on his bedroll on

the hard earth, settled his head on his saddle and tucked his blanket about him. Many times in the past he'd cursed his landlady's lumpy bed, but it had been the king of beds compared to this. The bedroll didn't protect him from the humps and bumps beneath him. He sighed, thinking again that Bill Mayfield was trying to get rid of him for ever.

He lay uneasily aware of Steve moving on the other side of the fire. He was cleaning and oiling his guns. The fire crackled as more wood was flung on it. It sounded far louder in the night. He wondered whether the flames would attract nocturnal animals out on the prowl. That thought made him sweat, but he calmed himself with the thought that Steve was there on guard.

Later, he awoke and was surprised that he'd slept at all. Steve was bending over him.

'Wakey, wakey! Breakfast's ready and the sun's up!'

Robert struggled on to one elbow

and sniffed bubbling coffee. It made his guts growl.

Breakfast over, they packed everything away and Robert learned to stow everything in its right place on the pack-horse. He learned the finer points of saddling up and hitching the animal's girth-straps, so that they were comfortable, yet not too slack.

'You've got to have an understanding with your horse, kid. He has to trust you, then you'll be able to trust him. It's important to remember that. He's your buddy. It pays off in a crisis. He can save your life on occasion. A few pats and gentle handling will make him your pal for life!'

Robert nodded and tentatively stroked the mare. She snorted and blew her nose and Robert jumped back. It was all right for Steve to talk. This one looked like a devil and was acting like one.

Steve laughed. 'You're sure touchy, kid. You're a stranger to her yet. Give her a few days, try giving her some sugar and she'll soon come to you hoping for a handout.'

Robert took some of the crude brown sugar and held it out on his flat hand. Sure enough the mare sniffed his hand, then curled her lips gently and scooped up the sugar crystals. It felt strange, her lips were soft and damp and used so delicately. Impulsively he put a hand up to stroke her long nose and she danced back, not yet sure of him.

It was then that Robert fell in love with her.

'Before we ride on, Malko,' Robert knew now, by his using his name, that this was going to be serious stuff, 'I'm going to give you a lesson in shooting. I've shown you how to take your guns to pieces and clean the parts, now I'm going to give you some tips on shooting itself.'

Robert shuddered inwardly, remembering the convulsive pulling of the trigger when he'd shot his first man. It had been a wild shot, done in panic. Now he was expected to deliberately focus his sights on a man and shoot him dead.

'Steve,' he began hesitantly, 'do I have to? I mean, I'm a reporter not a gunman. I'm a looker-on, not looking for trouble. I'm to write about what I see and do. I'm not likely to get mixed up in other people's fights.'

'You think you can roam the West and not get into someone else's fight? Don't kid yourself, Malko. You'll be part of the scene, part of the action and if you can't shoot straight, then you're dead meat! Believe me, I know!'

Meekly, Robert followed Steve well away from the horses and found a likely target area. There were the remains of a dead tree, blasted sometime in the past by lightning, Robert presumed. Steve eyed it carefully, and strode across to it and fixed a torn-off piece of his shirt-tail to the trunk at eye level.

He grinned as he came back to Robert.

'It'll be the nearest thing I've had to getting my shirt-tail blasted! Now, we're

105

going to try at twenty yards and then fifty and then as far back as we can get. You don't have to hit the cloth, just hit the trunk and see how much out you are. Some men are born good shots, others have to work hard at it. Let's see how good your eyesight is!'

Robert spat on his hands and fumbled for the gun in its holster. Steve rolled his eyes towards heaven but did not comment. It would have put the kid off if he'd mentioned his clumsiness. He sighed inwardly. It would be a miracle if this kid survived long enough to go back to the city.

'Right! Now make sure you've spun a bullet into place'

Robert did as required and then legs apart, he held the gun with both hands to steady it. Shutting one eye, he fired and missed the target altogether. He swore as the bullet twanged away in the distance. His ears rang, and savagely he spun again. He'd hit that goddamn cloth or at least the trunk if he stayed here all day!

Steve, watching him closely, was pleased to note his anger. The kid had the makings. He had spunk. He'd be good when he got used to regarding his gun as an extension of his hand.

'Try using one hand!' he called. 'Take a snap shot! There might be a time when you're handling two handguns. So get used to the feel of it!'

Robert braced himself; the gun was heavy, at least six pounds but he was surprised to find that he'd nicked the trunk. It showed up light against the outer grey bark. He took heart. As Steve lounged, lighting a cigarette and giving him terse instructions, he found himself getting closer and closer to the cloth.

Then finally, the cloth was shredded and Robert gave a whoop of joy.

'Nothing wrong with your eyesight, kid. It was a matter of getting used to the feel of the gun. You're beginning to handle it without being conscious of it. That's part of the secret of a gunfighter. He uses his weapon as part of himself.

It's his pard, his lifeline. It sleeps alongside him at night. A man gets used to his own guns and if he loses them or trades them in, he becomes vulnerable. It takes time to break a new gun in. I know. Once, during the war, I lost my gun and I grabbed up a weapon from a dead soldier. It was like as if my hand had been cut off and I was using something without life. A strange feeling it was and I sure thought in the days ahead that I should be shot.'

'But you survived!'

'Yes. I reckon I turned that new gun into an extension of my hand pretty sharpish. A week, and I forgot about my old pard.' Steve laughed grimly. 'I was sure scared shitless during that time, but I wanted to live and a man goes through hell and high water to live when he wants to badly enough!'

'You must have a lot of stories to tell, Steve.'

'Yes, but I never dredge them up, kid. I say never look back or all the ghosts will come back to haunt you.'

Robert nodded, thinking of the man he had shot. He shuddered. He didn't ever want to shoot another man. All these shooting capers were to please Steve, not because he expected to be in any situation that might need quick-firing skills.

'Well, I think you've done good for a first time, kid. I reckon if you practise at each campsite, you'll be fairly efficient by the time we come up against Falco.'

Falco! Robert had nearly forgotten the outlaw. Never having met him or knowing anything about him he had become a phantom.

'You think we'll find him, Steve?'

'Not think, know! It's only a matter of time. I'll find him if it's the last thing I do! He's a murdering bastard. Killed a whole family back in Virginia and blew up a train with his men as well as robbing banks further west. I've followed that bastard's trail long and hard. He circles around like a hornet buzzing here and there. This is the first time ever that he's only got a couple of men with him and the best chance I've got of catching him. So, yes, we'll find him, kid, you bet!'

There was the faint sound of pawing hoofs on hard dry ground and Steve swung around. Robert was vaguely aware of the speed with which Steve pulled his gun from his holster. His hand had been just a blur.

Then he was looking with surprised eyes at the ring of men surrounding them both. Indians! They were watching them intently, curiously and waiting for orders from their chief. They were sitting easily on barebacked horses. There must have been ten of them and Robert was scared enough to wet himself.

Steve raised his right hand.

'How!'

The chief, only a young man, scarcely more than Robert's age, lifted a hand in reply. Then he eased his mount forward and gestured at the tree trunk.

'Why you waste bullets on dead tree?

Tree do no harm.'

Steve laughed easily and some of the tension went out of Robert. Steve gestured to Robert and all eyes turned to him.

'He is young. He needs the skill that goes with a gun.'

'So he can shoot to kill?'

Steve's smile slipped a little. 'He needs to know how to survive in the wilderness, just like your young braves do.'

'This no wilderness. This our home!'

'Of course.' Steve bowed his head in agreement.

'You teach young brave to kill Indians?'

'No . . . no! Far from it! We have no quarrel with you! But there are bad white men and the boy must protect himself.'

The young chief sat awhile, ruminating, and Steve managed to whisper quietly to Robert:

'Don't panic. It's a hunting party. They're not painted for war.'

Then the young chief surprised them. He pointed south.

'Bad white men make war beyond yonder hills. Dead men lie waiting for carrion to pick their bones. Watch for the vultures flying overhead.' Then he leaned forward across his pony's neck. 'Have you coffee, sugar, whiskey?' His eyes gleamed at the word whiskey.

Steve sighed inwardly. They could spare little coffee or sugar but when needs must . . . He dismounted and began opening one of the saddlebags on one of the pack-horses. He fumbled inside, bringing out a small bag of brown sugar and a small box of coffee.

'Coffee and sugar, no whiskey.' The young chief's face fell but he eased his pony closer and Robert could smell the peculiar scent of buffalo fat, fresh sweat and a sweet odour he couldn't recognize. Later, Steve told him it was the smoke from sweetgrass that the braves purified themselves with and burnt to invoke good hunting from the Great Spirit.

Now Robert was taking in everything he could about the young chief, the colour of his skin, his blue-black hair cut raggedy about his shoulders and held back with a band of rawhide with an eagle's feather stuck in it at an angle. He looked at the deerskin pants, the strings of wampum about his neck and the little leather pouch, the armbands and, particularly, the broad leather band across his body and over his shoulder, the neat leather quiver that held his arrows and then at the bow, six feet in length. He imagined one of those arrows slicing through his leg and shuddered. A hunting-knife hung at his waist and he could see that they'd made a kill, for drips of blood seeped through the thong holding the knife and was staining his pants. He must remember it all and write it down at the first opportunity.

The chief took the sugar and coffee and without a word, kneed his pony. He turned and swiftly rode away, his men with him, without a backward glance.

Steve looked at Robert.

'You all right? You look pale.'

Robert grinned self-consciously.

'It was a bit of a shock. I wasn't expecting Indians. I thought at first I was going to be scalped before I'd sent my first assignment back East.'

'They weren't painted for war. When you see an Indian all daubed up like a totem pole, then you're in trouble. He's letting the world know he's on the war path.'

'What's a totem pole?'

'A pole made from a good sturdy tree, carved with the heads of the gods of water, fire and earth and also ancient medicine men who protected the tribe in days gone by. It is usually standing in a sacred place near the village where all the ceremonies take place.'

'Like an altar?'

'Something like that. It brings them good luck and watches over them and woe betide the tribe if the thing is destroyed by enemies. That would demoralize them. Small totems are good-luck charms and can be worn around the neck along with those little leather medicine-pouches they wear around their necks.'

Robert nodded. He remembered the little pouch about that chief's neck.

Steve was packing up his bag of staples.

'Good thing I remembered to keep a small supply of coffee and sugar ready for such an occasion. It's always a good thing to be one jump ahead. Always be ready for the unexpected!'

Now his face became grave.

'It looks mighty like we're going to have to investigate those dead men. Maybe we'll find Falco's body and the job's done before it's got started!'

Robert nodded. Gee, his next report back was going to be a humdinger! First the account of the Indians. He would have to spice it up a bit. He couldn't just say the Indians surrounded them quietly and went away with just sugar and coffee, like some passing cowboys. He wondered whether he could mention a tame cougar running at the chief's pony's heels. Then thought that was a bit too much to swallow. Mabe he could make it a wolf cub . . .

Then he thought of the dead men and the buzzards. That would make good reading. It would impress Bill Mayfield, especially if he put in some lurid descriptions about the dead bodies! He couldn't wait to get to the site and see everything for himself.

But his imagination hadn't visualized the reality and horror of the scene. He was sickened by the rotting smell and the obvious attack on the bodies by wild animals, the tearing of the flesh. There was the angry buzzing sound of flies vying with ants to fight their way into orifices such as eyeballs, nostrils and mouths. He turned away to vomit. God! This beautiful majestic wilderness could be a hard cruel place!

Steve, his face tight, mouth grim, turned the bodies over to identify Falco. At last, disgustedly, he stood up.

'Whatever went on here, Falco wasn't in it, or if he was, he got away.'

Robert, head down, swaying a little, was staring at a dark-red puddle, dried up but still attracting a bevy of ants.

'I think there's signs of blood over here, Steve,' he called.

Steve strode over to take a look. He didn't seem to notice the vomit that was already attracting the flies.

He squatted on his heels and poked the congealed blood with a stick.

'Yep, it's blood all right, but is it Falco's?' He stood upright and thoughtfully walked around the clearing until he came to the soddy tucked away in the hillside. Then he saw the carcasses of the wolves. One, whose muzzle was stained with blood, had been half-eaten, no doubt the blood had attracted some predator like a coyote, judging by the ferocity of the rending of its flesh.

Quickly he looked inside the soddy. In the gloom could just make out a makeshift bed, a rough table and a stool. There was a pile of badly cured skins lying in one corner. The smell was bad and Steve was glad to get out into the clear air. There were signs of blood in the doorway. Steve reckoned a hunter had been set upon by marauders and he'd put up a good fight, but was it his blood in the doorway?

He changed his mind when he followed the blood-drippings from the soddy to the small stand of trees and found the milling tracks of horses. Whoever had lost a lot of blood had got away. One of the bodies out there was the owner of the soddy.

Whoever had lost a lot of blood had managed to climb a horse, let loose the others and ride away. The tracks led south.

Steve returned to Robert who was now scribbling in his notebook to distract himself from his suroundings.

'We'll be on our way. We'll have to follow those tracks yonder and find out once and for all if we're chasing Falco or some other poor son of a bitch. Whoever he is, he won't be able to travel fast or far.'

'What about the bodies? We can't just leave them!'

'Hell, kid, we're not undertakers! We haven't the time for any planting. Anyway, it's better to let nature take its course. Birds and animals have to be fed. At least they make a good job of stripping the meat from the skeleton. Then it will finally come apart and in time the bones will sink into the ground.' He saw Robert shudder. 'Come on, kid, face up to things. We live close to nature and nature knows best when your time comes!'

Robert nodded his head slowly and went off to mount up. Steve was a cold unfeeling son of a gun, but somehow Robert wouldn't have him any other way. At least Steve would fight for him and protect him if push came to shove. He hoped to God it would never come to that.

Slowly they moved on, Steve's eyes raking the ground as they went for signs of the man they were seeking. Steve concluded that, whoever he was, was in a bad way. The horse ahead had been hobbled many times as if the man aboard had had to rest to gather his strength. At this rate they should catch up with him soon.

The sun was sinking, lying in low in the west when Steve pulled up in a small basin where a fire could be lit that wouldn't be seen by curious eyes after dark. There were surrounding bushes and several shade trees. Just the place to relax, for Steve was aware that Robert rode in discomfort. No need to hurry now. Their quarry couldn't be so far ahead.

A small fire was quickly lit. Soon the frying-pan was in action and the smell of panbread filled the air. Coffee was set to bubble amidst the flames and Steve did mysterious things with jerked beef, pounding it with the handle of his Bowie knife and adding water from his canteen into the small blackened pan. He threw in salt and spice from the small bags he carried and the combined smells made Robert feel more hungry than he'd ever been in his days living on the streets of New York.

The meal left them both drowsy. It also made Robert's inside work and muttering something about a man's got to do what a man has to do, he made his way into the bushes, undid his trousers and squatted. He belched, licking his lips and wondered whether he could ever concoct such a good meal as Steve did out of nearly nothing.

Then he heard the unmistakable rattle of a snake. He froze. Frantically he looked about him, not daring to move. The pile of new dung was already attracting flies and he felt several bites on his bare buttocks. He caught his breath and held it or he would have screamed.

Then, from behind a small rock, a flat head appeared, swaying from side to side, catching Robert's mesmerized eyes. Slowly it rose showing the dull silvery scales. It undulated with that fluid graceful movement that was so deceptive. Its long probing tongue flicked out as it sensed prey nearby.

Robert's blood ran cold. He'd heard of rattlers, but this was the first time he'd come face to face with one. He was sweating hard, drips of water fell from his forehead.

'Don't move a muscle.' The cool voice came from behind him. Vaguely Robert was conscious of his exposed buttocks. 'I'm aiming for him over your shoulder so don't flinch or I'll take your arm off!'

Robert gulped. He couldn't have spoken if he'd tried.

He waited and waited. The rattler's head moved like a pendulum. Then, just as Robert thought he couldn't stand it any longer and the rattler's head was swaying above its many coils, a blast from Steve's gun shattered the silence. The head, with its wide mouth and darting tongue, exploded into a vile mass of pulp.

Robert was deafened in his right ear. It was as if he was inside a bell that vibrated constantly. He toppled forward and hit his head amidst the dirt, his ankles trapped in the folds of his pants.

Steve hauled him upright.

'You all right, kid?' he bawled.

Robert heard him as if he'd whispered. He wiped sweat and dirt from his face and nodded.

'Then wipe your ass, son, and let's get some rest. You should know better than to squat down before looking around for pesky critters like that one! You should always keep your gun handy!' He walked away, laughing to himself.

Humiliated, Robert did as ordered. He pulled up his pants and followed Steve. That was a lesson he would never forget.

It was well before dawn when they resumed the trail. It was as if Steve had cat's eyes in the predawn grey gloom.

'How's the ears?'

Robert's ear still buzzed but he wasn't going to admit it. It was improving. He could hear better, but he'd had trouble sleeping and when he did he dreamt of rattlers.

'Much better. I have to thank you for what you did. It took nerve. You might have missed him and he would have taken a bite out of me.'

'I was more worried about taking a lump out of you! If you'd lost your nerve, I could have killed you!'

They looked at each other askance, and then both laughed.

'It was sure not the time for you to go, kid. All I can say is that you've spent one of your nine lives!'

'How many lives have you spent?'

Steve shrugged. 'A few. I can never bring 'em to mind. I don't set much store by things that happened in the past. I live in the now.'

Robert looked at him curiously. Surely there must be some moments in his past he would want to remember? His parents or a special woman or a buddy? He decided not to probe. Steve was the strangest man he'd ever met.

They hit a main trail. It looked as if

whoever they were following knew his way and where he was going. The drips of blood had long since disappeared but now Steve was following the horse's hoof-tracks. They were still unmistakable.

The trail led to a straggling street of shacks and a store with JACKSON'S HARDWARE painted in crude letters, a general store with barrels of grain, shovels and brooms hanging outside to attract trade, and a saloon that just announced succinctly, PETE'S PLACE in three-feet-high letters over a high false front. At the end of the street was a white adobe church with a tall thin spire and a working bell in the belfry.

Several loungers watched their approach into town. There were several mounds of horse-droppings littering the dirt road. So, Steve presumed, this was a meeting-place for a bunch of men. A posse or a gang? That was the question.

Steve's eyes glinted and he became watchful. Robert stared at the makeshift cabins disdainfully, comparing them with even the meanest hovels in New York. Jesus! How could folk choose to live this way? How did they survive the winters?

They pulled rein in front of the saloon and hitched their horses to the crude rail. Steve stretched as they climbed the steps up on to the veranda that ran round the establishment. Steve noted that the rocking-chair was still moving, as if someone had gone inside when they'd entered the town from the other end.

So whoever was inside was aware of their coming!

The batwing doors swung back with a creak and the two men moved into the gloom of the saloon. It smelled like one of the worst dives Steve had ever been in.

Both paused to adjust their eyes and then saw a stockily-built man behind the makeshift bar. He had the shoulders of a giant and the arms of a gorilla but he appeared short, not more than five feet tall.

He was already handing down a bottle and two glasses and a welcoming smile split his bristly features.

'On the house, stranger. Welcome to Pete's. I'm Pete and all strangers get the same treatment!'

'I'm no beholden man,' Steve answered evenly. 'I pay for my drinks.' He tossed a coin on to the bartop. 'For me and my buddy.' He proceeded to pour two drinks. He thrust one into Robert's hand with a meaningful look, then tossed his off and poured another.

Robert stared down into his drink. He wasn't a whiskey man, he preferred beer and Steve knew it, and why the peculiar glance? He decided that Steve had smelled something fishy amidst the smells of stale beer, sweat and the umistakable whiff of men's piss.

He sipped his whiskey and felt the heat in his stomach. At least it stiffened his nerve against the sudden qualm of fear as he turned and saw several mean-eyed men sitting at the tables. Four of them had been playing poker but had now stopped, as if turned to stone. The others looked tense, not the way men should look when strangers rode into town.

'Seems like you've been busy around these parts,' said Steve easily, nodding at the batwing doors. 'Outside there, the horses have left their calling-cards.'

The barman scowled.

'You're mighty sharp at coming to conclusions, mister. Why should it interest you?'

'It don't. Just making talk, is all.' Steve poured another drink.

'Then what brings you to our neck of the woods?'

'Hasn't anybody told you it's dangerous to ask questions?'

'Just making talk.' Pete reached for a dirty towel and started dunking dirty glasses into a bowl of water that looked like soup. Then he wiped them dry, leaving dirty smears.

Steve tried to count the glasses. So that bunch of men hadn't been gone long. He estimated there must have been at least ten of them.

'Any ranch hands wanted around these parts?'

'Nope! Hank Jordan is the big-timer around here and he hires only specialist men for certain jobs. You don't figure to be qualified for the kind of man he takes on.'

'Oh? And what kind of man is that?'

'Now it's you who's asking dangerous questions! How come you're buddying up with this youngster? He doesn't have much to say for himself.'

Robert, who'd been eyeing up the joint, mentally describing it for his notes, turned sharply. He was angry at the contemptuous tone.

'Hey! Watch it, mister! I know when to talk and act and I know when to watch and listen. A talking man never learns!' Robert gave Pete a look that he hoped was ferocious.

Pete drew in a sharp breath. The kid had come to life. There was more to him than he'd realized.

'Sorry, kid. I might have known you

wasn't one of these country bumpkins! Seen a bit of gunplay, have you?' Pete asked carelessly.

'You might say that,' Robert answered, thinking of the man he'd shot.

'Well, then, am I right in thinking you two are pistoleros?' Pete's smile grew wide now.

Steve frowned, not liking the way things were going.

'Could be. We can take care of ourselves. Why?'

The man grinned.

'You kinda had the look of one, mister. Now him,' nodding at Robert, 'I'm not sure of. A young rooster, mebbee, all piss and wind. But then again, you'd hardly have him for back-up if he hadn't got *cojones*!'

Robert's arm and fist jerked. He wanted to punch the fat smart-mouth but Steve's hand held him back.

'Hold it, kid, he's prodding you, to see how far you'll go.' He spoke calmly and clearly. 'If this dog's turd wants to try his hand, it's me he'll face up to!' He glared into Pete's black eyes.

'Oh, so he's your pretty boy, then? You don't want him hurt, eh? Hey, fellas! Come over here and see this pretty boy!'

Suddenly the silent watching bunch of men had surrounded them. Steve's face tightened, his lips drawn back in a wolfish snarl.

His hands blurred as his twin guns slipped from his holsters and he waved them around, aiming at chests. The men drew back and the beginnings of lascivious anticipation turned to sullen fear.

'The first man who moves, gets it. Pete here gets the next slug!'

The men all took two steps backwards and waited.

'Now fellers,' Steve went on, 'we mean you no harm. All we want is information and we'll be on our way. Anyone seen a feller called Falco around here?'

There was the sudden hiss of breath from one of the men at the back of the group. Steve pricked up his ears and one Peacemaker was trained on a mean-faced man.

'You feller, you've heard of Falco?' The gun clicked as Steve pulled back the hammer. 'I'm an impatient man when I'm wanting information, friend. So if you've seen him, tell me right now or else . . . '

There was a sudden rush to get away from the man as if the crowd was expecting trouble. The tall gangly man gulped.

'A man called Falco is at Jordan's place. He came in two nights ago. He had a ripped arm and was in a bad way.'

'Thank you. You've taken the twitch out of my hand, mister.'

'Just why do you want him, buddy?' asked Pete, leaning a little way over the bar, his hand stealthily closing on a bottle. 'Are you two rangers or bounty hunters?'

132

'Nope! But you're right to say we're after him.'

The bottle came up and the mighty strong arm crashed it down where he expected Steve's head to be. He missed and the swing of the bottle hauled him over the bar. Steve leapt out of the way, twisting, and shot the top of his head off.

There was uproar. Robert dragged his gun out and started to shoot, the smell of cordite in his nostrils. He was aware of other shots, Steve's gun booming beside him, another couple of men crouching and returning fire, but both shots had hit the ceiling in the sudden outbreak. He saw two men go down and blood splashing the wall and the batwings.

In the mêlée, it was hard to focus but then two men were coming at him, gunbarrels aloft as if intent on braining him. Suddenly Robert was back in the saloon in New York where he'd learnt to survive. His fists closed on two shirts. He pulled and the men jackknifed forward. As they did so, Robert leapt, legs apart and aimed for their crotches. He felt the impact from his feet shudder upwards to his spine. He fell, rolled, and was up again, tripping up a man who was trying to brain Steve.

He caught another man on the jaw with a haymaker that jarred him up his arm and into his head. Exultation sent his adrenaline spiralling. This is what he knew best, pitting wits and expertise with brawling fighters. He was in his element. A crack to the jaw, and an unsuspecting cowboy folded up, eliminated from this dust-up.

He saw Steve going down, kicking and flailing his fists at two men in front of him and one clinging to his back, choking him. Robert leapt to his aid using the sides of his hands and chopping at their necks as you would to kill a jackrabbit, then kicking them smartly as they rolled away in agony.

For a moment he stood breathing heavily, the pain in his hands subsiding. He watched as Steve threw off his attacker. The man catapulted at Robert, who measured his distance and, as the flailing body came at him, he caught him on the jaw. The man hit the far wall with a mighty crash.

Steve grinned. He had a black eye and a cut lip and blood oozed from a shoulder graze. Suddenly they were alone, with bodies lying in grotesque attitudes around them.

'We never actually stood back to back fighting, but we sure do make a good team, pard!'

Robert felt a warm glow slice through him. He detected a certain respect in Steve's voice that had been missing before. He held out his hand and Steve shook it. He looked around the saloon. Only two heads could be seen peeping around the door of the kitchen, those of a Chinese cook and his helper. The rest of the company lay motionless.

His gaze lighted on the remains of Pete and the splashes of blood around him.

'I guess they'll have to change the

name of this place. It's not Pete's place any more! Come on, kid, let's get out of here.'

Steve snatched two bottles of the best whiskey, dumped them in his pockets and walked out without looking back.

Robert followed, now aware of bruises and aching joints, but it had been worth it. It had bolstered up his self-esteem. He wasn't exactly useless in this strange new world. He could hold his own and Steve now knew it.

'I could have done with some grub,' he grumbled.

'Don't fret, we'll make out, but at the moment I want to watch the saloon. I bet you a dollar someone comes out and makes off out of town. Someone who'll mebbe lead us to Falco. Those bastards in there recognized the name. My guess is he'll make for Hank Jordan's place, wherever that is.'

Robert could only marvel at the way Steve got into other men's minds, for sure enough, a bowlegged cowboy staggered out of the saloon, looked furtively up and down the street, then headed for his horse. Soon, he was galloping out of town and Steve reckoned it was time to follow at a distance.

6

Hank Jordan sat back at the table inhaling his cigar, his eyes scrutinizing Jake Falco shrewdly. What was his *real* game? What was behind all that garbled explanation he'd come up with?

It had been ten years since he rode with Falco. A lot of sand had been blown hither and thither since those wild days. He was now the owner of a ranch, inherited after a shootout at a gambling table and, thanks to his foresight and nerve, had doubled its size.

He didn't need ghosts from the past.

'So,' he said now, 'why come to me? Why not use your own men for the trip to Mexico?'

'Like I told you,' Falco lied again, 'my men are on another project. Besides, I don't trust them.'

'You must have a lot of hardcases if

you can't trust your own men! What about the man you say stole your map? Was he one of your men? It seems to me you're slipping, Falco! I would have thought you would have had more hold over the sons of bitches!'

Falco squirmed in his seat and took a huge swallow of his beer. Resentment flared in him. Who the hell was Jordan to pass judgement on him? Just because he was now boss of a clearly profitable ranch didn't mean he could open his big mouth and say what he liked! He needed Jordan's help, more than the rancher knew, but if it hadn't been so important, he would have up and shot him for those words.

'Look, I've offered you a fifty-fifty share in whatever is stashed away. Isn't that good enough for you? I can't lay it on the line any better for you. Take it or leave it.' Falco held his breath, hoping his attitude might wet Jordan's greed for gold.

'Mexican dollars, you say? How did you get the map in the first place?'

Falco's eyes flickered. He hadn't expected all these questions. All he wanted was Jordan's expert advice on getting down to Mexico in one piece and to eliminate that scumhound Caulfield along the way. There was no map. He'd have to think of a good excuse if they killed Caulfield and found no map on him. Still, he would worry about that all in good time.

The important thing was not to let Jordan know that he had no gang, that they'd been killed off after a trap had been set by that railroad agent, God rot him!

Jordan's watchful gaze noted the flicker and the hesitancy of his reply. This ghost from the past needed watching. He was sure now that Falco was trying to use him.

It would be interesting to give him enough rope to hang himself.

'I got the map from an old prospector. He was dying. I found him in the badlands and I gave him water and — '

'Held his dying hand, did you?' mocked Jordan. 'Or did you shoot the poor old digger and rob the body?'

Falco remained silent. He wasn't sure whether Jordan was disapproving or if he went along with what might have happened.

'It don't matter how I got it,' he finally answered truculently. 'I got it. That's what is important.'

'Mmm, I'll have to think about it. It means leaving the crew managing the ranch. You know the saying, when the cat's away . . . '

'Then you don't trust all your boys?' Falco asked sharply, deliberately needling Jordan.

Jordan shrugged. 'Some. Some I don't.' He frowned. 'If you're thinking of propositioning them behind my back, don't. I don't take kindly to two-timers!'

'I wouldn't dream of it,' said Falco with deadly calm. The ratfink could read his mind!

'As I said, I'll think about it. Now

would you like a whiskey to chase the beer?'

He busied himself in pouring drinks for them both and sat back, ruminating. The whiskey sharpened his brain. Then he said softly:

'You never answered my question about the man who stole your map. Who is he? I have a feeling that you're frightened of him. Am I right?'

Falco's head jerked up. Now Jordan was going too far, probing old wounds, stirring up old hatreds. Jordan had always been good at prodding nerves. He bared his teeth in what should have been a smile but wasn't.

'Same old Jordan! Same poking and pressing to get a reaction! I know your style, buddy. Rake around and the truth pops out!'

'I'm not your buddy!'

'Buddy or not, I've given you a proposition and if you don't like it, then that's the end of that and I'll move on tomorrow.'

'Just as you like, Falco. I still don't

know the name of the man me and my boys would be chasing, and you haven't told me how come you've got your arm bandaged. Have you already had a run-in with him?'

'No, dammit! It's not a bullet wound. I was savaged by a wolf, if you must know! As for the man, his name is Caulfield, Steve Caulfield.'

Jordan sucked in his breath. He knew that name. Two of his pistoleros had had a run-in with Caulfield. They said he was a formidable gunslinger and they spoke of him with the respect one professional has for another. But would a man like Caulfield steal a map from a wanted man and run? No, the bastard would have killed first, and he certainly wouldn't have hightailed it down to Mexico, like some two-bit owlhoot.

Jordan reckoned the tale about the map was a cover up. Falco wanted him and his men to go after Caulfield and kill him. If that happened, what would come next?

He knew the answer to that. There

would be a showdown between him and Falco and, depending on surprise, Falco was hoping to take over his gang and his place, and eventually his ranch. He should kill him where he sat opposite to him, except that it would make a mess for his house-keeper to clean up.

Jordan stood up abruptly and stretched. The old clock on the wall struck twelve times as if on cue.

'Midnight. I'm going to bed. I'll give you my decision in the morning.' He left Falco sitting at the table wondering about his next move. His arm pained him. It throbbed and was red and swollen under the rough bandage. That goddamn wolf must have had poison on its fangs.

He stood up, grabbed the whiskey bottle and staggered off to bed. At least he was having another night's rest in a comfortable bed. God knows when he would do it again. He would douse his arm in whiskey and drink the rest and hope that Jordan would go along with his plan. One good thing, Jordan didn't know that Falco was alone and was the hunted quarry. He bared his teeth in frustrated rage. He'd expected that Jordan's greed would make him jump at the chance of sharing a stash fifty-fifty. He forgot that Jordan was now a rich rancher and had his own methods of adding to his wealth, and he certainly didn't know that Jordan had heard of Caulfield and his reputation.

He spent a restless night. The bed was too soft. The stale air of the room was suffocating and his arm gave him hell.

He was up before dawn but found Jordan and his men already up and preparing to ride out. It looked as if the sonofabitch had other things on his mind besides the sudden appearance of an old buddy.

It smelled like dark and dirty business. The bustle and organizing reminded him bitterly of his lost gang and the mornings they'd set out on a raid.

He strode out into the yard, intent on finding Jordan.

'Where's the boss?' he asked a passing cowboy who was carrying a saddle and heading for the corral.

The man jerked his head. 'In the arsenal, yonder,' he grunted and walked quickly away.

Arsenal, eh? Falco was impressed. Jordan sure knew how to organize. He walked over to what looked like a barn but wasn't. He stepped quietly. One of the double doors was ajar. He looked inside and briefly saw the barrels of gunpowder, the racks of rifles which now Jordan was taking from their racks and handing out to a bunch of his men.

The door creaked and Jordan looked up sharply. For a moment anger swept over his face, to vanish as quickly as it had come.

'Ah, Falco! Come on in! Meet some of my boys. This is Falco, an old buddy of mine, fellers.' Falco became the focus of attention.

Falco didn't like the keen-eyed

glances. He felt a certain resentment towards him. It was as if these strangers knew all about him and didn't like what they'd heard.

'Howdy,' he muttered, and stepping forward took down one of the rifles from its rack. He saw it was well oiled and was one of the latest Spencer repeaters; there must have been fifty of them, at a guess. 'Nice one.' He grinned at Jordan who took it from him.

'Yes, you might say that. I only buy the best!' He looked long and hard at Falco. 'I expect you're wondering what's on the cards today?'

'You might say that,' Falco answered cautiously, 'but it's none of my business.'

'Too right. We're off to see a man about some cows. Want to come along? We could use an extra man.'

'What about my deal? Have you thought on it?'

'Mmm, I'm afraid it's off, Falco. I don't need that kind of business. I appreciate the offer, buddy, but I've got my own set-up,' he said mockingly. 'I'm not the wild young hellion I was in the days I rode with you. You'd better find someone else with more guts than brains! Now get out of here! This place is off limits!'

Anger tore at Falco. It was a long time since anyone had stood up to him. The smirking onlookers didn't help matters. If he could, he would have shot the lot of them. He turned without a word and headed for the cookhouse. At least he would grab some coffee and fill his belly before he rode away.

It was while he was drinking the last of his coffee that he thought of the idea of following in the gang's tracks. His tracks would mingle with theirs and perhaps he could get far beyond Caulfield's search for him. He hoped to God the gang were heading south. That would be a great help, but wherever they were heading would get him away from the gunman.

He saddled up and rode out of the yard. Jordan, watching him go so easily, wondered what the bastard had in mind.

Steve and Robert, camping high on a ridge over-looking the Jordan ranch were up and eating a cold breakfast. They couldn't risk a fire so they ate bread and cold beef and drank water from their canteens.

They had followed the lone cowboy the night before to what was presumably Jordan's ranch. Now they watched the busy scene below.

'It looks like old man Jordan is on the prod again,' Steve declared, looking through his field glasses at the men below. Robert, chewing on a piece of tough beef, was hoping for a look. He'd never used a telescope or glasses before.

'Can I look?' he asked.

Steve handed him the glasses. 'Go on, take your time. It's not Jordan we're interested in. We only want to know if Falco is amongst them.'

Robert studied the scene below.

'There's a feller come out of that big barn. He's walking over to the cook-house. Oh, and a whole bunch have come out of the barn loaded up with guns and what looks like ammunition. D'you reckon they're preparing to ride out on a raid?'

'Could be. Let's have another look.'

Robert handed over the glasses and Steve watched the bunch of men. He studied them carefully and recognized a couple of professional gunmen.

He was in time to see a rider heading away from the ranch, a scout, possibly, under Jordan's orders to spy out the country they were heading for.

He was disappointed at no evidence of Falco's joining Jordan's expedition. He could have bet his last dollar that Falco would seek out old buddies, and though Steve had had no run-in with Jordan, he knew of his reputation as a suspected outlaw. So, they would have to cast around for any other leads.

He looked regretfully at Robert.

'Well, kid, it seems you're going to see quite a bit of new country before we catch that scumbag. It'll sure be good for your experience but hard on your ass! We'll head for the next town and ask around and if there's a telegraph office, you can get rid of those notes you're scribbling!'

It took three days to come to Louisville. They were now in the heart of Kentucky and still heading south. The Kentuckians were a hardy breed and the town bustled with the comings and goings of both settlers and those just passing through.

Fist-fights and barroom brawls, which ended up in the long straggly street, were common, raising dust along with that of carts and buggies and horsemen bringing in animals for sale. A runaway steer, frightened at the smell of blood at the cattle abattoir, rampaged amongst the crowd, knocking down unsuspecting bystanders, and charging head down amongst a crowd who were listening to an impassioned preacher. Gunfire could be heard in the background.

Robert was enthralled by the spectacle. Steve only grunted when he remarked on how exciting it was.

'Watch yourself! You're acting like a greenhorn! Keep your hand on your gun! There's those out there who'll take the gold fillings out of your teeth and you won't know it!'

'I haven't any gold fillings!'

Steve looked at him and grinned.

'Just a saying, kid. When you get as old as me, then there could be truth in it. I think we'll try that saloon over there. It looks a likely place to hear all the gossip and who's new in town.' He pointed to a two-storey wooden building with the words, THE SILVER DOLLAR painted in foot-high letters on boards running along an outside veranda.

They tied their horses to a hitching rail and went inside. A honky-tonk piano was being played by a thin white-faced man who coughed consumptively as he played. A row of beers was lined up on the piano top.

The room was dark and cigarette smoke hung about in clouds above tables crowded with drinkers and card players. No one looked up as they entered. All were too busy drinking and talking or intent on their poker-game.

'Two whiskeys and two beer chasers,' Steve ordered. He turned to lean against the bar and look over the crowd. The fat barman quickly served them and leaned over to Steve to ask quietly:

'Any news from the courthouse?'

Steve looked at him, curious.

'Not that I know of. Should there be?'

'They've been in there all the morning. I thought it would be cut and dried and the villain be strung up by now. That's why we've got such a crush of folk in town. Everyone wants to watch the hanging.'

'Hanging? We're strangers just got

153

into town. What's been happening?'

'Oh, you don't know! Yesterday we had a rare old howdy-do. A bunch of fellers rode into town and held up old man Rafferty at the bank, but the crafty old feller was ready for them! It appears that only he and his two clerks knew about the new safe and how it was rigged, so that if it was broke into, a charge of gunpowder would blow the safecracker to hell! By God it worked too! Mind you, it blew away a part of the bank as well. Old Rafferty wouldn't figure on that! He's mighty mean. He won't like having to pay to have the place rebuilt but at least they never got what he had stashed inside! Oh, yes, it was very entertaining, I must say.'

'Were there casualties?'

'You bet! Three dead and some at the door injured but those waiting outside carried them off. One man was found knocked out and he's the guy in the courthouse. The townsfolk want some entertainment. If the judge doesn't give the right decision, we'll string him up too, and the marshal if he wants to take him to the county jail. I think old Rafferty will get his way. The judge owes him money!'

Steve finished off his whiskey.

'It sounds as if we should hang around and watch the spectacle. Haven't watched a good lynching in years!'

The barman frowned.

'It's not a lynching, it's a hanging, all tight and legal, what with the judge and a sworn-in jury.'

'Call it what you like, but if the outcome's certain as you say it is, it looks very like a lynching!'

The barman shrugged his shoulders and moved away to serve a thirsty customer. Robert looked at Steve a little uncertainly.

'Does it matter? After all he was a member of the gang.'

'So they say. But they found him knocked out. It doesn't look as if the sheriff's tried to find witnesses that he's a member of the gang.'

Robert nodded.

'I suppose he could have been a bystander who got bushwhacked for some private reason.'

'Now you're really using your head, kid. I've known many a poor bastard tricked and blamed for something he didn't do and he swung for it! It's not a pretty sight to see a man's neck stretched and to have doubts as to his guilt!'

'What can you do about it?'

'Not a damn thing! If I was to protest too much about the speed of the justice meted out, I'd be in danger of being part of the gang, and so would you!'

Robert shuddered, his imagination tightening a rope about his neck.

'Do we have to watch it, if it happens?'

Steve looked mockingly at him.

'Why, sure, kid! It's part of your education! As a reporter on the *Tribune*. Don't tell me you haven't the nerve for it! You're going to see far worse scenes further west than a little old hanging!'

Steve watched Robert's face pale. It amused him to shock this kid. After all, he was doing him a good turn. It was all part of the toughening-up process.

Suddenly there was a yelling and screaming outside and several gunshots blasted the air. There was a rush for the saloon doors and men erupted outside.

'Guilty! The verdict's guilty,' a stentorian voice called out, laughing. Some of the men cheered.

Steve and Robert joined in the crush and were soon swept down the street towards the courthouse, which stood opposite the white adobe church. The street had widened into a square. One ancient shade-tree spread its branches above a rickety bench where old men usually sat and smoked and talked. Now the bench was empty of old men but a noose hung from one of the thick branches.

The courthouse door opened and three men hustled a struggling prisoner down the steps, his blood-soaked head covered with a dirty bandage. They were followed by the judge and the members of the jury. The crowd made way for them and an expectant silence fell. It was as if all those who were waiting to see a peepshow suddenly realized this was for real.

The prisoner was hauled up on the bench. As the noose was placed about his neck he started to thrash about, catching one of his jailors a mighty kick in the crotch.

The man howled and jackknifed on to the ground. A burly bearded man in the crowd dived for the prisoner's kicking legs and enveloped the man in a bear hug, imprisoning his legs.

'You or one of your God-cursed buddies killed my brother!' the bearded man shouted.

He gave a great heave and the prisoner was swung high in the air.

'Pull!' the big man roared.

The noose tightened as many hands dragged on the rope and the twisting body danced in the air.

For a long moment the body swung and gyrated, the eyes bulging and the tongue protruding. The face turned black. Then suddenly all movement in the legs ceased and only the creaking of the tree branch made any sound.

The body swung like a pendulum and the crowd stared fascinated. Then, gradually, as the blood-lust cooled, the men looked at each other a little shamefaced. It had all happened so quickly.

In ones and twos, the crowd dispersed, some to go back to their drinking, others to deal with those friends and relatives who'd died during the raid.

Soon the square was empty but for the ghastly sight of the body moving and eerily twitching as if somewhere inside it, there was the semblance of life.

Robert felt sick.

He wished he was back on the mean streets of New York. At least they didn't string a man up without giving him a fair trial. He cursed Bill Mayfield for sending him West. Someday, if he ever returned to New York, the first thing he would do would be to punch Bill Mayfield to the ground and to hell with the consequences!

But now he had to write a graphic account of what had happened. He would entitle it, *Rough Justice*.

7

Steve reckoned they needed another drink to get rid of the bad taste in their mouths.

'Come on, kid, another whiskey will put the colour back in your face! Just think of it this way, the sonofabitch had it coming to him. God knows what he got up to in life, even if he wasn't guilty in this case! Forget it! Put it behind you. Now let's go and have another drink!'

Inside the saloon it was again crowded and all the talk was about the hanging. A few pessimists were reckoning the bank-robbers would avenge the hanging.

The barman grinned as Steve ordered two whiskeys.

'A great show, wasn't it? Nothing like a hanging to bring the folk into town. Good for business,' he finished cheerfully as he placed the drinks in front of them.

'What about a room for the night? You're not full up, are you?'

The barman winked and leered at Robert.

'Only way you get a room here, mister, is with a woman thrown in. We don't cater for your kind!'

Steve leaned over the bar and grabbed the man by his shirt-collar, and twisted. The man was choking and turning red.

'Watch your mouth, buddy! Any more of that and I'll smash your teeth in!' He flung the barman back against his shelves of bottles and glasses. Several bottles fell to the ground and smashed.

A few bystanders turned to watch the scuffle but no one came to the barman's aid. He scrambled to his feet, hands in the air.

'All right! All right! You come in here with a young whippersnapper and ask for a room. What else should I think? If you want a room, as I say, it's one man and a woman to a room. You can take your pick. We've all shades and colours. We've got a nice young Mex, who'll do anything you want, and a part-Indian squaw full of fire, and a couple of beauties, sisters they are, with a touch of the tarbrush, and a gal from back East . . . '

Steve interrupted him.

'That's enough, feller. We're not hankering after women. We'll go and find us beds elsewhere. I guess there's a good hotel in this here town?'

'Yes. Two blocks further along. Run by old Rafferty, the banker. A mean old bastard, but he runs a clean house, no fleas, and baths if you want them!'

'Much obliged. Sorry I roughed you up, but you shouldn't jump to conclusions. At least you keep good whiskey!' With that, Steve turned and shouldered his way out. Robert followed, a bit disappointed. He would have liked to look over those fallen doves, as his father used to call them. He hoped

Steve was going to widen his education when the time was right.

They managed to get a double room at an inflated price. It was small and shabby and the two beds were lumpy, but at least they were clean. Steve took a look around and nodded.

'Not bad. Beds could be better but we'll be on our way tomorrow. Now let's go and get the horses settled. I noticed the livery stable a bit further along. We'll get them groomed and fed and watered and then we'll do a bit of asking around and see if anyone's heard of Jake Falco.'

The liveryman was obliging. He would groom and feed the horses and give them extra oats. Furthermore, he had a youth who dossed down in the stable overnight to watch out for prowlers. It would be a dollar each extra but well worth it.

Steve paid up cheerfully. It was one of the things Robert liked about Steve, his concern for the welfare of his animals. Casually, Steve asked the man about Jake Falco. Had Falco ever been in this town?

The man blinked.

'I know the name. Outlaw, isn't he? Hasn't been seen in these parts for three . . . four years. There was a spell when there was a lot of shooting up homesteads and the railroad track that was being laid was blown up. I thought he must be dead by now.'

'Nope! Unfortunately he's still alive.'

The liveryman's eyes grew keen.

'You looking for him? Are you a marshal?'

'We're looking for him. He's wanted in two states. I'd keep your eyes and ears open if I were you. He's been reported in this area.'

'Hell's teeth! We don't need no more trouble in this here town! One hanging's bad enough! The sheriff was only complaining about an hour ago about all the paperwork he's to get through, for the raid on the bank! We want new folk to settle here, not be frightened away with the threat of violence!'

'Well, I'm warning you. I can't do more than that.'

The man scratched his bristly chin as he watched Steve and Robert walk away. Then he called after them:

'How long are you going to be in town?'

Steve turned. 'Overnight. Less if we get on the scumbag's trail!'

They came to a small eatery, called Betty's Cabin. They could smell a mixture of stewed beef and chilli and Robert's guts rumbled. Inside, a small fat woman with grey wispy hair came to meet them, a smile on her face.

'Now boys, what can I do for you? I got beef stew and hash browns, or chilli beans and corncakes with sweetcorn and there's peach pie to follow. What's your wish?'

Steve raised his eyebrows at Robert.

'What's it to be, kid?'

'Stew and peach pie!'

'Right, make it for two, Mrs er . . . '

'Just call me, Betty, love. Everyone calls me Betty. I ain't ever been married, is what!' She bounced away and disappeared through a door which presumably led to the cookhouse.

A young girl brought coffee and gave Robert a sly smile.

'Just sing out if you want more coffee . . . or anything else you might want.' She gave him a wink as she went off, waggling her hips.

Robert wanted to smile but frowned instead. Steve didn't seem in the mood for any frolicking around.

The food was good and eventually Robert sat back, belching a little. He was in need of some exercise. He thought of the unknown girls in the saloon. He was in the mood for a bit of fraternizing. It could be a long night.

'How about taking a walk around and I could get me some ideas about this one-horse town and write about it. Bill Mayfield's bound to be interested in it when he reads about the hanging.'

Steve smiled down at him.

'It'll take all of half an hour to look

around, and then what do you think we'll do?'

'Have a drink somewhere,' replied Robert innocently. 'Maybe call in at that saloon and . . . ' he coughed and went on, 'maybe talk with some of them there gals. What d'you think?'

Steve laughed out loud.

'You're a little 'un, but you're game! A cocky little pilgrim! What makes you think those gals will even consider you?'

'Hell! They say it's not the size of the rider that wins races but the size of his whip!'

'Is that so?' Steve considered him through narrowed eyes. 'You're not actually telling me, you're one of those Don Juan fellers?'

Robert shrugged carelessly. He wasn't going to let on to Steve he'd only had one woman and she'd been a bit of a let-down.

'I've had me moments,' he said and stared Steve straight between the eyes.

'Well, well! Then let's get ourselves to that saloon and pick us a couple of females and maybe you can teach me something about how to treat a whore with style!'

'Hey now, I never said — '

'You either have or you haven't, kid, and I want to see how you go about chatting a female up and getting her up into one of those rooms that have to be shared! I'm going to be mighty entertained one way or the other!'

Robert was beginning to feel that he should have kept his big mouth shut. He didn't like being laughed at and God knew how he would handle a tough female who could punch a feller down if he didn't come up to scratch. Not like the young girls back East. The barman saw them coming and had the whiskey bottle on the bartop along with two glasses.

'Changed your minds? Want some entertainment?' The mocking glance he threw at Robert made him want to shove his fist in the man's face.

'You might say that,' Steve drawled. 'What have you got on view?'

'As I said before, we've plenty to choose from. If you go through that door there, I'll give Jenny the word and she'll see you right. Jenny's my woman and she looks after the womenfolk.'

Steve and Robert looked at each other, Robert's heart thumping, then followed the barman through the door behind the bar into a fetid passage which smelled of dampness and cheap perfume. It was dark and only a streak of light coming from under a door made it possible for them to walk easily.

The door was locked. The barman knocked and it was a few minutes before the door was opened by a breathless female of about forty.

The barman gave her a nod. She looked beyond him at Steve and smiled. 'Come this way. They're all together in here, those who're not working, that is.' She gave a tired smile and Robert, following Steve, could smell her stale sweet sweat.

His heart pounded. He'd never been in a place like this before. His introduction to sex had been in a back alley.

The room was lit by several oil-lamps. When Robert's eyes adjusted he saw several couches with tables, a couple of dirty Mexican rugs on the wooden floor and a long bar. Already there were several men present, drinking and laughing with the girls.

They all looked up when Steve and Robert walked in and Robert couldn't take his eyes off the girls. They reminded him of flowers, some grouped together, a mass of different-coloured flowers. Others sat with a partner, beside him or on his knee. Delicate hands stroked the bristly cheeks and suddenly he got an itch he couldn't scratch.

Then, as Jenny took them slowly around and introduced them to the girls who were alone, Robert saw that the girls were women, hard-faced and with disillusion in their eyes. They smiled with their mouths but those eyes remained dull, uncaring. Flowers? No, not flowers, just weeds dying at the edges, he thought and the itch disappeared. He wanted to get out of that stuffy stale-scented room.

He looked at Steve. He was talking easily to a young Mexican girl, who might have been pretty a few months ago but now her profession showed in her face.

He noticed they all wore low-necked gowns that caught the eye. Designed no doubt to catch a man who'd not seen a woman for months. Also he noticed that the finery was dirty and stained. One opulent creature's bodice had split showing a dirty white linen shift. All wore garish colours as if to make them stand out from each other.

He felt a hand caress his neck. He looked sharply around and saw a female nearly as old as his mother would have been,

'Hi, big boy! What about buying me a drink so we can talk and get to know each other?'

The badly dyed hennaed hair, the

thick white paint on her face to hide the smallpox scars and the hard scarlet bow of her lips resembled a mask he'd once seen on a jester back in New York.

He pushed her away.

'Not now. I'm having a look around.'

Her face twisted in anger.

'Ratfink! I'm not young enough for you, am I? You'd rather have youth than experience! Well, let me tell you something, I could teach you things those bitches have never learned! I've slept with the best lovers in the land! I could transport you to heaven. I could — '

Suddenly her shrieking ceased as Jenny threw herself at her and punched her on the jaw.

The woman fell like a pole-axed steer. Robert watched mesmerized as one of the other women helped Jenny to haul her upright and hustle her out of the room.

A few minutes later Jenny was back and apologizing to Robert and the rest of the customers for the disturbance.

173

'I'm sorry, folks, for the disturbance. Sarah's been drinking again and she gets out of hand sometimes. Drinks all round, Carlo,' she said to the barman and hastily left the room.

Steve was sitting at a table with his young partner. He indicated a seat beside him. He looked at Robert with raised eyebrows.

'All right?' He laughed at Robert's woebegone face. 'Doesn't say much for your expertise with women. What set her off?'

Robert shook his head.

'I didn't want what she was offering.'

Steve shouted with laughter and took another gulp of whiskey.

'Holy mother! Don't you know better than to refuse them to their face? I thought you had experience! If you don't fancy them, you buy them a drink, tell them something fancy about how they remind you of your sister or your mother and you revere them too much to have more than mere conversation! Slip them a dollar because they remind you of your folks and they'll drift away. It's hard cash they're looking for and they've got a dollar nice and easy. That's how it's done.'

'Oh!' Robert nodded. 'I'll remember in future.'

Steve laughed again. He was in a teasing mood.

'You're not a Don Juan after all. I wasn't at your age,' he went on more seriously. 'I remember giving myself a great reputation with the ladies, and one of them caught me out. It was humiliating. But she put me through my paces eventually and I've always had a soft spot for Milly Adams. I used to visit her for years when I was passing through Cincinnati.' He sighed. 'A great woman, heart of gold. Always made me welcome. Yes, one in a million.'

'What happened to her?'

'Got herself killed in a street brawl with another woman.'

'Gee, that was awful! Did the woman kill her?'

'Nope! Her lover did! He wanted the

175

other woman, see? But the crowd strung him up and stretched his neck.'

'And the other woman?'

'Took over Milly's place, refurbished it and made a fortune!'

Robert digested this quietly, not sure whether to believe everything Steve told him. It would make good reading if he could slip it into his accounts of his adventures. He could alter the woman's name . . .

He was thinking deeply about what he should write when Steve nudged him.

'Watch out! There's going to be trouble soon!'

Robert looked around. All seemed quiet enough.

'Why do you think that?'

'Look over yonder at that table in the corner. Two men sitting with two females, and watch, there's two hopefuls walking over to muscle in.'

Robert watched as two determined women, a blonde with hair dressed high, wearing a pretty but soiled blue gown with dirty white flounces around the neck, and elbow-length sleeves, came to stand at the table with a hand on her hip. A raven-haired buxom wench in purple-and-gold stripes, stood by her. They were smiling down at the men as if they knew them. The blonde even bent and kissed the man nearest to her.

The men were looking up and laughing with them. Robert watched the original two girls growing mighty uneasy.

He was fascinated. He wished he could hear their conversation.

Suddenly one of the seated girls stood up and slapped the blonde's face.

'See, I told you so,' said Steve with a chuckle. 'When it comes to barroom fighting, you can't beat women. They go for the jugular!'

As Steve spoke, the other girl stood up. Her chair crashed over as she leaned over the table and walloped the second interloper. The battle was on.

The two men's laughter turned to

panic and both dived out of the way as the women clashed. The table was overturned and those sitting close by scattered, giving the girls plenty of room for the catfight.

Robert noticed that most of the other women left the room in a hurry but the men stayed to watch what they reckoned to be entertainment. Bets were being placed, the men were laughing and cheering and urging the women on. To the amazed Robert, the women were a writhing mass of colour with arms and legs flailing. The sight of long, bloomered legs made him blink as did the uncovered bosoms as the fight went on.

Hair became unloosed and the blonde in blue was trying to choke the redhead in yellow with her own hair. He wanted to get in there and drag them all apart but knew he'd be in danger of his life.

'Why doesn't someone stop them?' he shouted in Steve's ear.

'Why should they?' bawled back

Steve. 'It's good entertainment! See how everyone's enjoying themselves!'

'But they're killing each other! They've drawn blood. They're trying to scratch each other's eyes out!'

'That's why they've got long nails! Didn't I tell you they're the best fighters in the world?'

'Jesus! I'd hate to quarrel with one of them!'

Steve grinned. 'All cats purr if you handle them right. Don't be put off, kid. There's always kittens to be found!'

Suddenly the door burst open and Jenny was standing there with a heavy Colt in her hand. She fired it twice into the ceiling and the shock of it sent the women rolling apart. They lay panting, scratched breasts heaving, torn gowns gaping, showing expanses of bare calves and torn-bloomered thighs. They were a sight to behold.

'Get up, you goddamn mad-brained sluts and get out! I'll deal with you later!' Jenny turned angry eyes on the menfolk. 'What you want for your filthy money? You want to see them kill each other? Why couldn't you have stopped them instead of just gawping at them?'

Someone laughed.

'Aw, don't be a spoilsport, Jenny! The girls loved it! It was only a little bloodletting and they let off steam! Look at them! Beauties all of them! What you say, fellers? Let's show we appreciate the show!'

All the men cheered and dollars and cents were thrown at the two women as they crouched on the floor.

Then the fight started again as they wrestled and struggled to snatch up the coins. Robert turned away in disgust as the men urged them on, their faces animated and cruel, like the faces of men he'd seen back East at cockfights. He moved to the door. He couldn't stay any longer. It would be a long time before he forgot this night. Steve saw him go. He followed and both were silent as they made their way to the saloon bar and ordered drinks.

The barman grinned at them.

'Some lively goings on in there.' He cocked his head towards the inner door. 'I wish I'd been in there to see it. Was it good?'

Robert turned away as if he hadn't heard the question. Steve took a drink and answered coldly.

'I've seen better fights amongst squaws at watering holes. Something to really scrap about!' He turned away from the grinning barman, who shrugged his shoulders and moved down the bar to serve someone else.

Robert downed his whiskey fast. He was getting used to the hot sensation in his stomach and quite liked the jolt it gave him.

'Let's get out of here,' he said brusquely. 'I've had enough of the nightlife.'

Steve tossed off his drink.

'Now you're talking. Let's go and hit the hay. It's going to be an early start in the morning.'

They strode the sidewalk in silence.

When they came to the hotel, Steve said softly:

'Diappointed, kid? It didn't turn out as you expected.'

Robert gave a rueful lopsided grin.

'I wasn't much in the mood anyway.' He knew he was lying. He had been, until he'd actually been faced with the reality of it all and the catfight had certainly put paid to any real feelings for it.

'Ah well, better luck next time. After all, it was a bit of a pigsty.'

'Yes, it was a pigsty, wasn't it? I'd rather have a good night's sleep!'

They turned into the hotel and the sleepy receptionist lifted his crossed boots off the counter, came awake and found them the key of their room. His eyes followed them speculatively as they mounted the stairs. Then he settled down again and, closing his eyes, began to snore.

★　★　★

182

Jake Falco had cursed his bad luck when the gang he was following rode towards the town. Hank Jordan had tried to fox him by saying they were going on a cattle raid, which Jordan had done many times in the past. Now the sonofabitch had brought his men into town and he, like a fool, had followed, like a maverick calf. He'd only realized they were mighty close when he smelled the odour of humanity wafting on the breeze, that mixture of cow-dung, man's open sewers and the stink from the town's rubbish tip along with rotting cow's heads and entrails and piles of bleaching bones. It was a mixture of stench that warned all travellers before they entered any growing town.

He'd found himself a hideaway where he could see but not be seen. He was high on a butte, his horse tethered far below and for three days he'd watched and suffered. He'd heard the gunfire and guessed the target was the bank. At first he'd wished he'd been with them to share in the spoils. Then, as the outlaws came galloping madly out of town after an explosion that shook the earth, some of them riding double, he was damn glad he was where he was, hiding out in a crack in the butte, which had turned out to be an old dried-up waterway. Water still seeped down through cracks in the rocks, but the ground hadn't known a rush of water for eons of time.

But the time had come when he was desperate. His wound throbbed and pain was now slicing through his fingers of his left hand. His old wound had now healed on his right wrist but he would never make a fast draw again.

His whiskey was gone, some of it used on his left arm, but he had been prudent and kept most of it to drink. His canteen of water was empty and the only food he had were strips of salt bacon which he chewed to soften them before he could swallow.

The time had come to sneak into town and find a doctor. He knew he had a fever and that he would die horribly if he didn't get expert attention.

So, he'd made the effort to ride into town. He'd found himself a doctor who proved to be an old man. He was also an alcoholic, which was obvious when he began to unwind the dirty strip of shirt from Falco's upper arm with trembling hands.

He whistled gustily between his teeth as he surveyed the swollen upper arm, noting the yellow pus edging the angry red flesh. He looked over his steel-rimmed glasses at Falco.

'Mmm, I'm more used to treating bullet wounds. This looks like you been fighting with a cougar? Animal bites can be more lethal than bullets. It's the germs in their mouths they get from eating rotten flesh.'

'I had a run-in with a wolf, at least it was part wolf and part dog.'

'What you been cleaning the wound with?'

'I had nothing but good liquor.'

185

'And just dirty rags to wrap it in. No wonder you're in danger of losing your arm!'

'Hell! It isn't as bad as that, is it?'

The doctor pursed his lips and sucked in his breath. He wondered just how much he could take this ignorant scumbag for.

The wound stank and it looked as though it was going rotten but, lanced and cleaned properly, the arm would be as good as new in a few weeks, even though the little weasel-looking feller would carry a scar for the rest of his life.

The doctor darted a glance at the man's thin pallid face. It must be causing him hell.

'Look, mister, this arm looks like a lump of raw meat gone bad. Now I've got to get rid of the poison. I'll have to cut the flesh, get rid of the accumulated pus and swab it. Now that costs time and money. You ready to pay, mister or are you wasting my time?' He bent over Falco, grinning, and his alcoholic breath swept over him, making him want to vomit.

'I've got the money. How much?'

'Let's see now ... I'll have to use a scalpel, expel the poison, sew you up, use clean bandages and my time and not forgetting a slug of whiskey for you as I do it. Let's say, ten dollars?' The doctor eyed him narrowly. 'Paid in advance of course!'

Falco breathed heavily. It was a stick-up but he had no choice. His arm pained him and the doctor's earlier words had frightened him. He'd rather be shot than die from a blasted wolf bite!

He fumbled in his vest pocket, drew out ten dollars and thumped it down hard on the doctor's battered desk.

'There you are, Doc, now give me a shot of whiskey and get going with that knife of yours!'

The doctor grinned again and poured them both a generous tot. He toasted Falco as he supped it off.

'Here's to you that the knife don't

slip. I'd hate to be the one who made you stiff!'

Great galloping toads! Falco thought, the feller's loco. What am I doing letting him loose on me? Then his arm gave a great throb and he closed his eyes. He had no choice, but he vowed that if the old sot made a mess of his arm and he lost it, and he lived, he'd come back and shoot the croaker between the eyes.

'Right, let's get at it! Get up on the couch and lie still and don't move or I might stick you in the wrong place.' The doctor busied himself getting towels and bandages ready while Falco settled himself on the leather couch.

Falco lay and watched him totter back with a scalpel and an enamel dish of water from a black kettle hanging on a trivet over a wood fire. The water was slopping over as he staggered to the couch.

'Now, are you ready?'

The bowl was placed on a chair and

the old man waved his scalpel in the air while Falco lay back waiting for the first cut. Then, smiling widely, the old doc seemed to make his mind up. He lunged forward as Falco shut his eyes tight.

The incision made him scream. His whole arm was on fire and the stench was indescribable. There was much grunting from the doc and then Falco fainted.

Gradually the blackness lifted and he found himself lying like a trussed chicken, his arm swathed in bandages. The doctor was sitting with another glass of whiskey in his hand.

When Falco tried to sit up, the doctor thrust a glass in his hand.

'There you are, an extra drink on the house. Keep the bandage on until tomorrow and then change it. I've given you some extra bandaging to keep the whole thing clean. You're all fixed up and you'll be fine in a few days. God willing!'

Suddenly there was a knock at the

outer door and a youth burst in.

'Hey, Doc, the jury's out. They're going to hang that outlaw right now! They want you down there to pronounce death when it happens! Jiminy! I've never seen a hanging! I'll see you in the square, Doc.' Then the youth was gone. The doctor turned to Falco.

'Well now, I don't expect you're in the mood for watching no hanging, so sit yourself here until you feel like moving and then just shut the door behind you. There's no need to lock it. It's never locked.' Then he whispered, 'You paid me well, have another whiskey on me and take your time,' and he was gone.

Falco rested himself and took advantage of the doc's generosity. Before he knew it, the doc's bottle was empty. He grinned to himself. The old devil would be as mad as hell when he saw his empty bottle.

For a while Falco sat hazily comfortable, as the throbbing eased in his arm. Then, curious, he looked about the office, saw the skeleton on a hook in the corner of the room, examined some stomach-churning sketches . . . surely his insides didn't look like that! Feeling revolted, he wanted fresh air and thought it time to go and see who was entertaining the town by hanging. It occurred to him that he could possibly know the victim.

Unsteady on his feet, he made his way to the square where he could hear whistles and catcalls. Hiccuping a little, he joined the outskirts of the throng. Stretching up to his full height could just see the swinging rope suspended from the tree in the square.

He knew the man swinging there. He'd laughed and drunk with him just a few nights before. He watched, detached. It was a mighty hard way to go. Still, it was his own fool fault he'd been caught. Falco turned away and then stood stock still with shock as he stared at a tall man who seemed to stand out from the crowd. Steve Caulfield!

He blinked. He must be drunk! It couldn't be Caulfield! The son of a bitch couldn't possibly be here. But he was. He watched the big man speaking to a little runt of a kid and waited to see what they would do.

His right hand twitched; his instinct was to shoot Caulfield before he was aware of him, but the jostling crowds put paid to that idea. He would have to play a waiting game and dry-gulch him out of town.

The shock sobered him. He would have to watch carefully and see which way Caulfield was heading, then ride ahead and find a likely spot to ambush him.

He wondered briefly about the kid. Possibly just an onlooker like himself.

But he changed his mind about that when Caulfield and the youth entered the saloon. They must be drinking buddies. Well, he'd soon make crow-bait of a kid like that.

He badly wanted a drink to steady himself but knew he couldn't risk

Caulfield recognizing him, so he fought the urge which was gradually turning him crazy because he knew he couldn't assuage it.

He collected his horse tethered outside the doctor's office and fed and watered it at the nearest ostler's. He'd be ready for a quick getaway out of town. Then, after tying him up outside the drygoods store he loitered along the sidewalk smoking and watching the saloon.

Then he saw the unmistakable figure of Caulfield emerge through the batwings along with the boy and walk towards the hotel. So they were not leaving immediately.

Falco cursed inwardly and risked getting closer to them, following behind a group of ranch hands laughing and joking about some catfight that had gone on in the saloon.

The ranch hands crossed the street. Falco pulled down his hat over his eyes, hunched his shoulders and followed in the shadows behind the man and the boy. Then he heard what he wanted to know. They were heading south in the morning! Falco smiled in the darkness. He'd be waiting somewhere on the trail for them!

8

Falco returned to his previous hide-away. It was as good as anywhere and from where he crouched behind a boulder he could see the trail winding over the scrubland. It was also a good place to watch for any deviation in the tracks going southwest. Groups of boulders and stunted trees would give cover if he needed to move in a hurry.

It was a long night. His sore arm kept him awake. He could make no fire that might betray him when morning dawned. He wanted it to be a complete surprise. He had no compunction in shooting Caulfield in the back; he prefered it that way. He was in no condition to challenge the son of a bitch to a gunfight, his stiff right hand put paid to that.

The sun came up over the distant hills and his anticipation grew. It was a pity Caulfield didn't realize this was the last day he would see the sun rise . . .

He drank water and chewed on the rest of his bacon, his belly rumbling for hard liquor.

Then his heart started to race. Two tiny dots were coming at a fair lick. So the kid was travelling with Caulfield. For the first time, Falco wondered who the kid was and why he should stick with the big man. Anyway, it didn't matter. The buzzards would soon feast on both of them.

He loaded up his rifle and hunched down, ready to take a bead on his moving target. Elated, he watched the two men coming nearer and growing larger. Soon, he would have to gauge his distance. There would only be one chance to take the scumbag out; after that, Caulfield would be on guard.

He glanced about him, making sure that if the unlikely happened and he missed his target, he could slip away easily, fork his horse and be away amongst the rocks and trees to try again further along the trail.

Now he could hear the pounding hoofs as the two horses made good time. If he was to get Caulfield he had to do it now, as they thundered along the dirt road below him.

He braced himself, his rifle following the line Caulfield's horse was taking. Twice he was ready to pull the trigger and twice he was foiled by the young kid riding a little ahead and covering both Caulfield and his mount.

Cursing softly, Falco waited. Then his moment came. Caulfield drew ahead. The scumbag was laughing as if the two of them were racing each other. He noted the youth's clumsy riding. Where the hell had he learned to ride in that manner?

But all thoughts of the kid left him as he leaned forward, concentrating on Caulfield. He pulled the trigger and felt the recoil, the air around him became wispy with gunsmoke. For a moment he felt elation. He'd got the bastard!

His elation was short-lived. He saw

the horse stumble and Caulfield's hat fly off and he knew with a sick realization that he had failed.

He shot again and again in his panic and watched the dust rise from the ground as Caulfield and the kid leapt for cover. He knew then that he would have to move and move quickly. Caulfield was no fool. He knew there would be only one man in this territory who would set out to dry-gulch him, and Caulfield's mother had been a bloodhound bitch!

Down below, hunkered well behind a rock, his horse galloping along the trail, Steve shouted to Robert:

'You OK, kid?'

'Yes, bruised but OK,' Robert shouted back in a shaken voice.

'Watch yourself. Don't raise your head, whoever's up there could be waiting to take potshots at us!'

'What about the horses?'

'Forget them, kid, They won't go far. Just concentrate on keeping your head down.'

'D'you think it's Falco up there?'

'Who else?' Steve answered grimly. 'Look, I'm going to crawl through that thick scrub yonder and make for the other side of that hillock. I'm going to try to get round and behind him, then try to flush him out. If you hear me yell, come out shooting for he'll be coming down this slope, lickety split!'

Robert gulped. This was going to be a hell of a story to send back to Mayfield, if he lived, that was.

'Right!' His voice wobbled. 'I'll be ready!'

'Don't be scared. He'll only come if I don't get him on the other side of this hill.' Then he was gone and Robert was alone.

He was sweating heavily, but he wasn't scared only excited. He was getting a rush of adrenaline that he'd never had before. This was better than brawling in a saloon! One reason was because he trusted Steve Caulfield and looked up to him. He hoped he would become like him some day.

He heard gunshots beyond the hill and he tensed. They came again at intervals and he knew a gun battle was in progress. What should he do? Wait as instructed or go to Steve's aid? Maybe he was being cowardly in cringing here. If he'd been older and experienced he didn't think Steve would have told him to keep out of battle. He reckoned Steve was regarding him as some helpless child who had to be protected.

He flushed at the thought. Hell! He'd never learn about the West if he took a back seat! He would climb up there and see what was going on! Falco wouldn't be expecting someone climbing up behind him, he reasoned. The son of a bitch would only have eyes for Steve.

It was hard to climb the steep incline but he made it and paused long enough to get his breath back. Then he moved cautiously forward, his Colt in his hand. God knew where his rifle was, he'd lost it when he tumbled from his horse.

Then he saw movement far ahead and guessed it was Falco holed up.

Gunsmoke wafted up into the air as slugs raked the ground below. Robert held his breath. Surely Steve was still OK? He heard answering gunfire as bullets pinged against the dusty earth around the great rock where Falco hid, and he breathed a sigh of relief.

Now he was in a quandary. What should he do next?

Then it came to him. If he could creep around to the back of Falco and climb on to the rock behind, he could drop on the crouching figure and stun him before he knew what was happening.

Robert liked that idea. He was more used to rough-house fights than using a gun. Yes! He would take him that way and it would show Steve that he was wasn't just useless lumber but was useful in his own way.

It was hard to move quietly but he managed it. Eventually, he raised himself on to the rock. He stood upright. He had to move fast or Falco could drill him through the heart as he jumped. He raised his hands and took a great leap, feet aiming at Falco's shoulders. They came down firmly and Falco went down, but he twisted as he fell and the rifle wavered, then dropped from his nerveless hand. Falco screamed as he rolled on to his wounded arm and then began to fight ferociously to shake off Robert, who was now trying desperately to hold him.

Soon, they were a mass of tangled legs and arms. Falco bit down hard on Robert's wrist, drew blood and then tried to gouge out his eyes. Robert swung at his jaw but missed as Falco squirmed clear. He took a jarring rap on the side of his head in return.

It had all happened so fast, and now both were gasping for breath. Falco's surprising ferocity was a revelation to Robert. Brawling back East was nothing to what these murdering scumsuckers could get up to! It was another lesson learned.

Robert became aware that Steve had

climbed the slope and was now with them. Then Falco brought the heavy rock he'd grabbed for and brought it down on Robert's head. Robert blacked out and never heard the shot that blew Falco's head off.

★ ★ ★

Robert groaned as he tried to move, his head was pounding as if held between two millstones and his skull was being ground to powder.

'Take it easy, kid, while I put a bandage on your head. You're bleeding like a stuck pig!'

Robert opened his eyes and found Steve crouching over him and doing things to his thumping head.

'What happened? I think a mountain fell on me.'

'Not to worry. Falco pulled a fast one and tried to beat your brains out!'

Robert put up a hand. He felt a makeshift bandage and the hot stickiness of blood. He groaned.

'How bad is it? I think my skull's stove in.'

'A hell of a bump and a cut. You'll live,' Steve observed crisply, noting the panic and fear on the kid's face. 'Think you can stand up now?'

He helped Robert to his feet. Robert swayed alarmingly as his surroundings started a giddy whirl.

'Where are we going?' he asked dazedly.

'Not far. I'm going to carry you to the other side of the hill. I've got a job to do and you're better resting away from it all.'

'You mean . . . ?'

'Yes, I'm going to bury Falco.'

'But you were supposed to take him in!'

'I can't with his head blown off! I'll take his boots and his guns and holsters for evidence and anything I can find to identify his body. The boss knows me. He'll take my word they're Falco's belongings,' replied Steve evenly. 'The reward will go to you.'

'Why me? You're the one who was after him. I only tagged along for the story!'

'Stow it! Keep quiet and get your strength back. We've got a long way to go!' With that Steve heaved Robert over his shoulder and carried him away to a small hillock under the shade of a scrawny bush.

Steve hurried away to do his grisly job. There was no way he could dig a grave in the hard ground for the body, so he searched around for somewhere suitable: a cleft in the rocky ground or a dip, which he might use. He found a crevice that might have been used as an animal's lair. It would do nicely.

He stripped the headless body of boots and gun holster, then searched for anything useful in the vest-pocket. He found a crumpled wanted poster, several dollars, a battered timepiece and a flat tobacco-tin which contained a dried ear, no doubt a memento of some raid.

Then he dragged the body into the

crevice and covered it with rocks until he had a fair-sized mound. He laid Falco's hat on the mound where his head should have been and stood back to survey his handiwork.

'There you are, Falco, you son of a bitch! You got more than you deserve, but I hope you roast in hell for all the pain and grief you caused in your lifetime!' He made his way back to Robert. He looked down at him.

'How you feeling now, kid?'

'The world's stopped spinning. I could do with a drink.'

'Good. Think you can ride your horse?'

'They're still with us? Yes, I guess I can ride.'

'It'll be tough, but we've a long way to go.'

Steve gave him a small shot of whiskey, then stood over him while he took a good drink of water out of his canteen. The boy looked less drawn. Steve was satisfied. The boy had grit. They would take it easy, make for the railroad and wait for a train going east. A thought struck him. He had to know Robert's plans.

'You'll have to come back east to claim the reward. Will you come back west again?'

Robert looked thoughtfully at him.

'It's not my reward, Steve. I told you that.'

'Must I spell it out, kid? That scumbag had me nailed down. We could have traded shots all day until we both ran out of ammo. He could have got away in the end! I messed up, kid. I thought I could creep up on him but he was smarter than I realized. He read my mind and was ready for me. If you hadn't jumped him, I would have lost him. That's the plain truth kid. You got him, I didn't!'

'I only thought to distract him, Steve. I really thought I'd bitten off more than I could chew. He was a good infighter. The fellers back East couldn't compare to him!'

Steve looked at him admiringly.

'It took guts to jump him. He could have turned on you before you jumped and shot you dead! Did you think of that?'

Robert smiled ruefully as he held his aching head.

'No, I didn't,' he confessed. 'If I had I wouldn't have done it!'

'Well, all I can say is that I'm proud to have you as a pard and I'll sure miss you if you choose to stay back East!'

'You mean that, Steve? I thought I was just a burden on you!'

'I sure wouldn't say it if it wasn't the truth. I'll miss you, kid!'

Robert heaved a deep sigh, then grinned.

'What makes you so sure I'm going back?'

'Well, you're an up-and-coming reporter. When you get all this stuff written down and printed in the *Tribune*, you're going to be famous!'

'Oh, to hell with all that! New York means mean streets and a cut-throat existence to survive. I like it here in the wide open spaces and I'm damned if I'm going to leave it! After all, I worked hard to learn to ride a horse!'

Steve laughed.

'You've come a long way since you took your first ride! Seriously though, I could get you a job on the railroad. I could do with a sidekick. It means hunting out criminals who concentrate on the freight trains, especially those bringing supplies or the railtrack gangs. How you feel about that?'

'Sounds good to me. I can always keep sending reports to the *Tribune*. The folks back East will always want to know how the railroads are spreading across the country.'

'Then we'll make for Washington and grab your reward. Then we'll take some time off and relax and,' now there was a twinkle in Steve's eyes, 'I'll show you some real class.'

'You mean what I think you mean?'

'Yes, kid. Not the mean dives like we were in before, but real classy joints where the surroundings are rich and we're waited on like kings and the girls are . . . how can I put it?' he kissed his fingers . . . 'like dainty flowers, all sweetness and light, who don't even know what a punch is! Oh, you'll love it and I'll tell you straight, kid, you'll go in there as a boy and you'll come out a man!'

They both laughed and Steve put an arm around him.

'First things first, kid. We got to get out there. There's a long trail to cover, but think of the girls and we'll sure get there!'

THE END